# Half Moon Harbor Resort

## Volume One

Marissa Dobson

Published by Sunshine Press

Printed in the United States of America

ISBN-13: 978-1-939978-34-9

# Contents

# Dedication

To my wonderful husband, Thomas, who reads my work even when he isn't a fan of the paranormal world. To Kelly Mueller for being there when I needed someone. You were always there with a word of encouragement, or a title when my creative juices were done for.

# Learning To Live

Meg Harper is tired of living in a box created by her overprotective brothers because of her ability to see guardian angels...

Jay Wilder a lion shifter so wrapped up in the guilt of not being able to save his friend that he might lose everything...

Can Meg and Jay save each other or are they destined to live half a life?

# Chapter One

Standing on the ferry, Meg's body sagged with exhaustion, a vacation was just what she needed. Renting a small cabin at the Half Moon Harbor Resort was just what she needed to get over this funk. From what she had heard, the Half Moon Harbor was the perfect place to forget about your troubles and find peace within yourself. The best part was there was no cell phone service. She planned to spend the week putting her life back together. She wanted to spend much of the time alone because she had things she needed to figure out.

She didn't tell anyone where she was going; she only told her family and close friends that she needed time to herself and that she would be unreachable for a week. As expected, they put up a fuss, demanding she tell them where she was going and what she was planning. She stood firm, not giving in to their demands. She didn't need one of her overprotective brothers following her.

As the ferry passed the half-way point, her cell phone beeped, letting her know she lost service. Relief flooded through her. Pulling her phone out of her pocket, she sighed with gratitude at the sight of no cell phone signal. She made it, she thought as she saw the resort coming into view. A whole week to herself; she wasn't sure what she would do with it, but she knew she needed it, just as she knew she needed the air she breathed.

As the ferry docked, she let most of the other passengers depart first. She had no desire to get too close to people this week. Dinner was going to be the hardest time to avoid them since the Half Moon Harbor only served dinner for the guests in the dining room. She wondered if she would be able to handle her ability then, and what she would do if she couldn't. She had never been around a large group at one time before. She tended to avoid situations like that at all cost.

Stepping off the ferry, she made her way to the reception area, wondering if she made the wrong decision by coming here. It was too late now; the ferry was already returning to the mainland, and wouldn't come back for a week. Half Moon Harbor had the ferry come weekly unless there was an emergency.

The woman sitting behind the desk looked up from what she was doing as Meg approached. "Hello. You must be Meg Harper. I'm Kathy. Welcome to Half Moon Harbor Resort."

Meg tried to ignore the motherly spirit that was hanging protectively by Kathy as she checked in. "Thank you. I have a cabin reserved." She tried not to be rude, but she could barely stand. She just wanted to settle into her room and take a nap.

Kathy retrieved the key for the cabin, but instead of handing it to her, she held it when she noticed Meg was looking strangely behind her. "What are you looking at?"

She merely stared, tongue-tied for a moment. "Umm…Nothing…Sorry, I was just lost in thought," she forced out. She bit her lip nervously. She was sure Kathy could tell she was lying, but what was she supposed to say? Oh nothing, just your guardian angel. People would think she was a nut. Whoever heard of someone seeing guardian angels before?

Kathy eyed her doubtfully. "You cabin is number three, it's right out those doors and down the path. Dinner is served in the dining room at six o'clock. Enjoy your stay."

\* \* \*

Settling into the cabin, she wondered who Kathy's guardian angel was. She always wanted answers to the questions that puzzled her, that's what got her in trouble. That's why she was here. She needed to figure out how to live with this ability, without letting it control her life. She was tired of living in isolation; she wanted to have a real life. Deep down, she wasn't sure if a normal life was possible; her gift made living like a normal person extremely challenging. Could she find a way to control it, instead of it controlling her? That's what she wanted to find out.

The cabin was stunning and the large fireplace made it feel homey. For a brief moment, she wished she had someone she could cuddle up by the fire with. She asked for their largest cabin, and this one had two bedrooms. She didn't need the extra bedroom, but she wanted the space.

The cabin had a small kitchen, guests didn't need much since dinner was served in the dining room and there was room service.

The rest of the open floor was for the living room and a small workout area off to the side.

She placed her suitcase in the master bedroom before returning to the living room with the bottle of wine she had brought with her. Before bed, she liked to have a glass of wine to help take the edge off the day. Seeing guardian angels tended to put an added stress onto everyday living, especially trying to hide the fact from others. She placed the bottle in the door of the refrigerator as someone knocked on the cabin door.

On her stoop stood six figures, only three of them were solid. "I'm Sarah, an owner of Half Moon Harbor Resort. May we have a moment of your time?" Kathy was standing there with her head down, looking uneasy. There was also a man with them that she didn't know. She assumed he was a guest, with his jeans and tee-shirt and a duffle bag slung over his shoulder.

She nodded and stepped out of the way, "Please come in." What else could she do?

"Kathy informed me there has been a mistake in booking for this cabin this week. It seems as though the computer booked you and Mr. Wilder in the same cabin for the same week, without notifying us of the mistake until he tried to check in."

"I'm not sure what you expect me to do about it. I'm already settled. Can't you put him in another cabin or in one of the guest rooms?" This was not how she wanted her trip to start. It could be a disaster for the whole week.

"I'm afraid not. Every room and cabin is booked. You're the only one with a two bedroom cabin."

"Absolutely not! There is no way! I came here to get away from everything. I'm not sharing a cabin with someone I don't even know."

Sarah stood there silently for a moment, radiating calmness. "I understand, but there is nowhere else for him to stay."

He had stood there letting the women speak, but he spoke up now, as if he knew that if he didn't do something fast, they would be sending for the ferry. He cleared his throat. "Miss, I know this is an inconvenience, but it was an overlook by the staff. I won't be in your way. I just need a place to sleep. Please." He looked as drained as she felt.

She let out a puff of air that made the loose hair around her face flutter. "Fine. You can use the bedroom, but please do your best to stay out of my way."

"Thank you," he said as he set his bag down.

Sarah looked as though she knew it would work out. "Thank you, Ms. Harper. Whatever we can do to help you enjoy your stay, please don't hesitate to let me or the staff know."

"Thank you. I just want to be alone. I need a nap and a shower before dinner."

"I understand," she said as she motioned for Kathy to follow her to the door.

Kathy hesitated before she walked through the door. "Ms. Harper, I am truly sorry."

When they were alone, the man closed the space between them. "I'm Jay Wilder. I know you aren't thrilled with the situation, and I am sorry. I will do my best to stay out of your way and make your stay here as enjoyable as it should be."

"Thank you. I'm Meg. I'm here to get away from it all. I needed space without people breathing down my neck." She rubbed the pendent around her neck before she continued, as if it gave her the strength she needed. "You can have the bedroom on the left. I already have my things unpacked in the master. I'm going to take a nap before dinner." She headed towards the master bedroom without waiting for a reply.

When she had the door closed, she rested her forehead against the door and whispered why me? All she wanted was a break. She didn't need a roommate. She didn't even have a roommate at home; dealing with someone around all the time was more than she could handle. Now she had to deal with a stranger sharing her cabin.

What was he? She wondered. His guardian angel was different. She knew vampires didn't have guardian angels that followed them, so that ruled that out. Plus it was still daylight. She was at a loss as what it could be. Could he be a shifter?

# Chapter Two

Slipping her sweater over her head, she heard someone knocking on her bedroom door. For a moment she was startled by it, then she remembered Jay.

She opened the door to find him standing there. His light golden hair brushed the collar of his olive green dress shirt. He was picture perfect. Too bad she wasn't in the market.

"I thought you might like to be accompanied to the dining room," he said with a dangerous sparkle in his eye. "You never know who you'll meet there."

"Be assured I can protect myself, but yes, I would actually love some company tonight." She was nervous about being in the dining room without being able to control her gift. Maybe having someone with her would help keep things from getting out of control.

As they headed to the dining hall, they made small talk. "Where are you from?" she asked as they neared the building.

"I recently returned to my hometown in Maine for a new position. Before that, I spent the last year traveling. Most of the time it's great to be back home close to my family, friends, and people I grew up with. You?" While he spoke of his hometown, she could see the joy in his eyes. She could tell he was a man that valued his family and friends.

"I'm in the Seattle, Washington area. But my family makes me want to move far away." She was surprised how easy it was to talk to him. She never told anyone her secret desire to move. Her family drove her crazy some days, especially her brothers.

"Oh, I know how it is when it comes to family. There are five of us and I'm the only boy."

She let out a light hearted laugh. "I'll trade you. There are four of us and I'm the only girl; three brothers, all older than me, who try to protect me from every little thing. I'm surprised they let me cross the street by myself."

"I don't blame them one bit. Brothers are supposed to protect their sisters. I try with mine, but they tend to gang up on me. When they have a problem, though, they all come running to me to solve it." He let out a small chuckle as he spoke of his sisters.

Her heart swelled with the love this man had for his sisters, why couldn't her brothers be that way? There was something that drew her to him, a desire she tried to deny. "I don't have a chance to ask for help. They have already solved whatever problem it is before I even get a chance," she said as he opened the door. "Don't get me wrong; I am grateful for my brothers, I just wish they would let me open up my wings and fly a little."

He didn't reply to that comment. For some reason, she had a feeling that he would take her brothers' side. He seemed just as protective as they were.

Walking to the dining room she had forgotten all her worries, but as they entered the nearly full dining room, her reservations were back. They were able to find a table close to an exit, as she preferred.

She tried to stay as lighthearted and carefree as she was on their walk over and concentrate on Jay, but all the misty figures proved to be too much for her.

"Excuse me," she whispered before making her escape. She could feel every eye on her as she bumped into a waiter in her rush. She didn't stop to apologize. The moment the fresh air met her lungs she felt better, a weight lifted off her shoulders.

"Meg, what's wrong?" Jay jogged to her side as she sagged to the bench.

"Nothing. Go enjoy your dinner. I just need some air." She couldn't look him in the face. The fact that she was lying was apparent all over her face, even in the dim light of the moon.

He tilted her head, making her meet his eyes. "Bullshit, Meg."

She barely knew him, but she felt the need to bare her soul. If only she could. What was she supposed to say? I see guardian angels and I can't deal with their demands. That made her sound like a freak of nature.

Hell, who was she kidding? She was a freak of nature.

"Damn it, Meg. What's going on? I can feel your pain. It's slicing through me." She could see the hurt in his eyes.

"I…umm…can't explain." A tear ran down her check. She didn't know what to say to him.

"You can, and you will. Come on, Sugar. Tell me." He wiped her tears away. "Nothing can be as bad as you think it is."

"I'm a freak," she whispered, her voice tight with tears.

"Why do you think that?"

Throwing caution to the wind, she blurted out, "Because I can see guardian angels. They want my help to lead people on the right road to happiness."

She tried to pull away from him, wanting to leave, but he held her tight. "That doesn't make you a freak. That makes you special."

People were starting to leave the dining room and their privacy was being interrupted. "Let's go for a walk."

He held her hand as he led the way to a path. They walked in silence until they were out of earshot. "Does everyone have a guardian angel?"

"Mostly." Her voice was still laced with tears.

"Have you ever come across shifters or vampires? Do they have them?" he asked as they came to the mystical lake. There were benches and old lamp posts giving the lake a safe, peaceful feel.

She stared at him in shock. She was careful who she mentioned paranormal beings to because those who haven't seen any with their own eyes aren't quick to believe in them. "Umm," she said, not sure how to answer that. How did he know about things that go bump in the night?

"You can't tell me you haven't come in contact with one," he said, eyeing her suspiciously.

"Maybe I haven't," she said defensively.

"Sugar, you're sitting next to a lion shifter. Do I have a guardian angel?"

Now it all made sense. He wouldn't see her as a freak when he wasn't normal, either. For once, someone might accept her for who she is. "Somewhat."

"Care to explain that more, Sugar?"

"You have something. It's like a ball of energy, but it seems to have animal characteristics. It's something that I have never encountered before." She stared behind him into what appeared to be thin air, with a puzzled look on her face.

"Have you ever seen this in a shifter before?" he asked, drawing her close to him as they stood by the lake.

"No. I've never been around shifters before. Vampires, yes, but my brothers are protective when it comes to shifters. They always kept me at a distance, never letting me get close."

For a moment, his eyes burned with anger, and then he let out a forced laugh. "Your brothers allow you around vampires but not shifters. Are they idiots?" His voice was controlled but showed hints of rage.

She pulled away from him, trying to get a handle on her hurt feelings. "Who the hell do you think you are, talking about my brothers like that? No, they aren't idiots. They are trying to protect their only sister. Just when I thought you were one of the good guys, you turn out to be a total jerk." She turned on her heels, heading back to the cabin.

He grabbed ahold of her arm, his grip tight, making sure she wasn't going anywhere. "Wait, Meg! That isn't what I meant. I only meant that vampires are just as dangerous, if not more so. Unless you forgot they like to dine on humans."

"I haven't forgotten, and they can control themselves."

Once again he let out a forced laugh, and then pulled down his shirt collar. "Really? Because my experience tells me otherwise." His temper flared. There was no holding back the rage in his voice, or the snarl from his guardian angel.

The wound on his neck looked vicious; she was surprised he had even survived. She reached a hand up to touch it. As her cool hand touched his warm neck, she could feel the anger he held slide away. She wondered what happened to cause the vampire to attack.

Before she had a chance to ask, he lowered his head and kissed her. His mouth covered hers hungrily.

He broke the kiss and stared longingly into her eyes. "From the first moment I laid eyes on you I wanted you. I need you, Meg."

Since she opened the bedroom door before dinner, she could feel the desire for him building in her, his kiss made it explode inside her, demanding to be let loose. The anger she had a moment ago dissolved and all she felt was the lust for him rushing through her body. She never wanted anyone like she wanted Jay at that moment. She nodded. She didn't think they could make it back to the cabin, but thankfully for them she noticed a blanket sitting on the bench. She didn't notice it when they came in, but it was there now and that's what mattered.

Grabbing the blanket, she led the way to a secluded place in the trees. While he laid the blanket out, she stood there looking anxious. She never did anything like this. What if someone stumbled upon them?

Oh who cares? She thought as she lowered herself to the blanket.

His arms encircled her, one hand on the small of her back as he brought her close. He looked as if he wanted to ask her if she was sure, but he saw no doubt in her face. He kissed her softly at first, then his kisses turned fast and furious.

Their lips broke apart when the clothes started to get in the way. As she worked the buttons of his dress shirt, he drew her sweater over her head. Their mutual desire was rushing them. She wanted him to be slow and sensual, but this was not the time. She secretly hoped there would be another time, hopefully in their cabin.

Pulling the shirt off his arms, she admired the toned body that kneeled before her. One hand slid down the taut stomach, tracing his abs. Before she could explore further, he eased her down on the blanket.

"Sugar, I want you," he growled.

"For tonight, I'm yours." She could get lost in his eyes. They reminded her of a sandy beach. One she could picture them making love on, just as they were in the woods.

He licked the side of her neck, lightly nibbling on her flesh; she knew he marked her with his scent. She almost expected to be upset about this, but instead it made her feel valued. As if this wasn't just a one night stand. Can I live in the same cabin as him for the next week if this is only a one night stand?

He drew her out of her thoughts with a kiss. Easing the lacy cup of her bra aside, he gently outlined the circle of her breasts. His touch was light and painfully teasing.

"You're beautiful," he said as he slid her pants from her hips, before slipping out of his jeans.

Left with only her bra on, she reached up to unhook it. "You're pretty amazing yourself," she said with a smile.

He was on her before she could blink. The heat of his body kept her warm against the chill of the night's air.

"I don't want to ask, for fear of the answer, but you want this as much as I do, right?" She could see his desire for her mixed with a fear that she would deny him when he was so close.

"I want this...I want you. More than anything else." Aroused now, she drew herself closer to him. Their lips met again; it was too late to change their minds.

His hands roamed intimately over her breasts as his mouth moved south, away from her lips. He kissed his way down her body, taking extra time with each nipple. They grew taut under his tongue. He teased her nipples with his tongue, drawing them between his teeth, making her cry out with yearning.

"I want you!" She moaned out.

She could tell he was taking his time for her, but she was growing impatient. She wanted him now. She was hot with desire and didn't want to wait another moment. If he was a human, she would have taken matters into her own hands by rolling him over. Being a shifter meant she couldn't roll him. Instead, she reached down and cupped his cock in her hands.

She worked her hands up and down his cock, making him hotter for her than he already was; she wanted him burning with desire. She tried to do it faster, but the angle was off. Instead, she worked it in a teasing fashion.

He growled out a plea. "Enough."

When she let her hand fall to the side, he positioned himself on top of her. Without warning, he pushed his cock through her tender flesh. A moan escaped her lips as her body exploded into a fiery sensation.

It didn't take long before their bodies were in exquisite harmony with one another. It didn't take them long before their arousal peaked, and the urgency picked up. She matched his urgency with her own lusty, unstated needs.

"Oh, Sugar," he whispered in her ear as the waves of ecstasy throbbed through her.

She cried out for release. Her breasts crushed against the hardness of his chest as he kissed her.

They lay panting, all their energy spent. If they were in the cabin, she was sure they would have succumbed to sleep as satisfied lovers often do.

## Chapter Three

Meg curled into the curve of his body, with her arm across his midriff. She didn't want this moment to end. She wanted to stay like this until they had the energy to make love again. Her head rested in the crook of his arm, her eyes closed as she thought about what led her to this trip.

His body went still; he lifted his head up as if he was listening to something. She didn't hear anything. "Get dressed."

She reluctantly did as he suggested. His whole body seemed on edge as he slipped into his jeans.

She had just slipped on her sweater when he pulled her close, blocking her body with his own. She didn't see the gun before, but it was clear as day in his hand now. She opened her mouth to ask him what was going on when a shadow stepped out of the trees.

In the light of the moon stood her brother, Matthew.

Shock yielded quickly to rage. "What are you doing here?" she yelled.

She lightly laid a hand on Jay's arm, and whispered, "It's my brother, Matthew." Instead of lowering the gun as she expected, Jay kept the gun pointed at him.

"I'm here to save your ass, as always."

She could feel her brother's anger from where she stood. "I don't need you to save me. I'm not in any danger."

Matthew didn't move towards her, or even look at her. He kept his eye focused on Jay. "Yeah, right. Do you even know what you're with?"

Jay let out a loud growl, one that would have frightened most people. Meg stood by his side with his arm still around her. "Matthew, this is Jay. How did you find me?"

"You're with a damn shifter, Meg. Now get the hell over here before I have to do something you might regret."

She tried to keep her anger in check, but she was failing miserably. Matthew always brought the worst out in her. "Matthew, this is none of your business. I'm a big girl. I can take care of myself."

"Not against a shifter, you can't," he yelled. She could tell he was ready to fight. No matter how many hours her brother put in at the gym, there was no way he would win if he went up against a shifter. Even if the gun wasn't part of the situation.

Jay had stood quietly by, letting Meg handle Matthew, but she could tell he was getting irritated. "I have no intention of hurting your sister."

"That's what all of your kind says."

"Stop this!" she yelled. "Matthew, it's about time you let me live my own life. I want to know how you found me."

"Dan hacked into your email and found your reservation confirmation. I booked a room at the resort so I could keep an eye on you."

Her computer savvy brother, Dan, didn't believe people had privacy online, especially her. She was frustrated beyond all belief. Was there no limit her family wouldn't push? No boundary they wouldn't break? Before she could really lay into him, two more figures stepped through the trees. It was Kathy, from the front desk, and Richard Brady, the head of security for the resort. She had met Richard when she was looking for the lobby earlier that day.

Richard spoke as Jay pocketed his gun. "Mr. Harper, I won't have your interfering with the other guests. I don't care if she is your sister." Before Matthew could interrupt, Richard turned to them. "Jay, take Ms. Harper back to her room. I will be by after I deal with him." She was thankful Richard said room, not cabin. Hopefully Matthew wasn't sure where on the island she was staying and she would still get some privacy.

As they were left the woods, Matthew didn't say anything, as if he knew he was outnumbered, and couldn't win against both Jay and Richard. Or maybe he realized he pushed Meg too far this time. Doubtful, she thought.

# Chapter Four

Back in their cabin her anger continued to mount. She was spoiling for a fight that had been interrupted by Richard. For once she wanted to have it out with her brother. She wanted to tell her whole family they were smothering her. She needed air, room to breathe, and they weren't giving it to her.

"Sugar, are you okay?" Jay asked, sinking into the couch next to her.

"No…Yes…I don't know."

He wrapped his arms around her, pulling her close. "I'm sorry you have to deal with this, Sugar. If you would like, I can go knock some sense into him," he said with a light chuckle; one that made her think it was what he would like to do, if it wouldn't hurt her more.

"I just don't understand my family's reason for being this way." She rested her head on his shoulder.

"You honestly don't know, do you?"

She was suddenly confused. He asked that as if he knew something she didn't. How could he when they just met? "Know what? Why they are acting this way? No, I don't."

He let out a puff of air and dragged his hand through his hair. "It's not really my place to tell you. You should ask your brother."

"You know something. Just tell me. My family hasn't told me a damn thing my whole life."

"Just don't shoot the cat that brings the bad news, okay?" He waited for her to agree before continuing. "I didn't know who you were until I saw your brother. Your brother, or I should say, your family, has history with the previous alpha of my people." He paused for a moment, turning so he could look her in the eyes. "There is no easy way to say this … your mother was part shifter; it was repressed. It wasn't until after she married and had her daughter that she realized it."

"Me?"

He nodded.

"Why me? Why not my brothers?"

"I'm not sure. All I know is that is when her animal characteristics started to show. The previous alpha was a cruel man. He demanded your mother leave her family and join our ranks. When she wouldn't, he had his soldiers attack. They were supposed to bring her back alive."

Knowing where this was going, she finished for him. "Instead, she was killed."

"Yes. Along with your brother, Jonathon."

"What? I don't have a brother named Jonathon."

"You did." He rubbed a hand up and down her arm. "I'm truly sorry."

She tried to let it all sink in, but it was so overwhelming. "Did you have anything to do with it?" she asked in a meek voice, scared of his answer. If he answered yes, then whatever they had going between them would be over before it started.

"No, I was only a child then."

She wanted him to hold her. She wanted to cry for the mother and brother she never knew. Because of what his people did when they were children, her family hated his kind. She had no hatred for him or his people, but could she ask him to live with her family's hatred just to be with her? Was she worth that kind of sacrifice?

"You should know the alpha is no longer in power. Shortly after what happened, my people found out and overturned him. Six months ago, I took over as the alpha, and I can ensure you nothing like that happens under my watch."

She could see the hurt in his eyes; feel the hesitation in his touch. "Jay, I don't blame you. There was nothing you could have done."

He looked relieved, but she could tell he held something back. She wanted to wash way his doubt. Make him see that nothing had changed between them, but the knock at the door put a hold on any plans she had.

# Chapter Five

Richard and Sarah stood at the door. "Ms. Harper, he is in his room for the night and should not be bothering you. If you have any more problems, please let me know."

She nodded, grateful to him for dealing with Matthew. She hoped this vacation would be a break from her family, but with Matthew here, it could turn out to be a disaster. Thankfully, she found Jay, or the whole trip could have been a catastrophe.

Meg moved out of the way to allow them to step into the cabin. She didn't want to stand there in the doorway in case Matthew could see the cabins from his room.

As if he noticed her fear, he tilted his head towards the resort. "His room is on the other side."

Her shoulders relaxed, but inside, her brain was telling her it wouldn't be long before he found out where she was staying.

Sarah held a tray with two milkshakes. "The staff was having milkshakes and I thought you would enjoy them. I find ice cream always helps to relieve stress. Also to help make your evening more enjoyable, here's a little gift bag from the gift shop. There is a bath salt and candle I love. They'll help you relax. I recommend taking a bath tonight to help let go of your anxiety."

Jay took the milkshakes, handing one to her before grabbing the bag and placing it on the table.

"Thank you. You have both been so helpful."

"You're welcome," Sarah said as they turned to leave. "Bethany asked me to mention she would like to see you in her yoga class tomorrow morning. As you asked when you made your reservation, I spoke to Bethany to see if she could help you with your ability. She thinks she knows a few tricks that can help. Talk to her tomorrow after the yoga class."

"I'll be there," Meg said with a nod before closing the doors.

"What shall I do with you now that I have you all to myself?" Jay said as he kissed the back of her neck. "First a bath, then you are all mine."

While she finished her milkshake, he strolled off to start the bath for her.

"Sugar," she heard him call from the bathroom.

She slipped out of her clothes, strolling into the bathroom without a care in the world. The bathtub was surrounded by candles, and the steam from the hot water was whisking up from the claw-foot tub. The whole bathroom smelled of lavender and rosemary.

"Your bath awaits, Sugar." He was still clad in his jeans, his shirt forgotten along the way.

Climbing in, she asked, "Won't you join me?"

"Not yet. I want you to relax, but I'll be back shortly to wash your back." He kissed her forehead and strolled out, leaving her alone with her thoughts.

The water was steaming hot, just the way she liked it. She rested her head back on the edge of the tub, letting her thoughts surround her.

What would Matthew do next to stop whatever was happening between them? She thought. She tried to anticipate his next move so she could plan hers. She didn't want her brother ruining what could be the best thing in her life. Even if it only lasted the week she was at the resort. She wanted to enjoy every moment of it.

All these years her family lied to her. They told her that her mother died in childbirth. They never told her about her other brother, Jonathon. She didn't understand why they didn't tell her. Why keep her in the dark? She wondered.

Then it hit her like a bolt of lightning. She sat up in the tub with such force, water spilled over the edge. They didn't tell me because I am a shifter. They kept me protected from others of my kind because of what it might do to me. That's why I was protected from every man who ever looked my way, not because they were trying to protect me, but because it could bring out the shifter in me.

She wanted to scream for the agony they caused her. I had a right to know, she thought as Jay came sprinting into the bathroom

"Sugar, I can feel your pain. What is it?" He sat on the side of the tub, cradling her face in his hands.

"Everything!" she cried. The tears streamed freely down her face, blinding her and choking her voice, as Jay pulled her out of the tub and into his lap.

"Sugar, I never wanted to hurt you. You deserve the world." He held her as she cried, rocking her gently.

"It's not you," she choked out between sobs.

"Tell me what I can do to ease your pain. Just name it, Sugar."

She could feel his longing to take away her pain. She could feel his guardian angel snarling with need. "Knock some sense into my brain dead family," she said, trying to lighten the mood.

A smirk formed on his face. "Sugar, I would do that in a heartbeat if I didn't think that would cause you more pain, and make you hate me."

"I couldn't hate you," she said softly as her body started to calm after her breakdown. "Just hold me for a moment."

"That I can do. I'll hold you forever if you let me," he whispered, locking her in his embrace.

# Chapter Six

He held her until she was ready for him to let go. She enjoyed the feeling of his arms and didn't want it to end, but they couldn't stay on the bathroom floor all night. He had to be wet from pulling her out of the tub.

She lifted her head up and kissed him. He returned the kiss and it was surprisingly gentle. She gave herself freely to the passion of his kiss. "Make love to me," she whispered.

He gazed at her for a moment before he swept her, weightless, into his arms, and carried her to the bed, laying her down gently and swiftly stripping off his clothing.

He joined her on the bed, their kisses became hot, as if they were trying to devour each other.

"Tonight I'm going to show you how special you are to me. I long for only you." His lips were warm and sweet, making her want them over and over again.

There was an intimacy between them she'd never felt before. One she was worried Matthew or one of her other brothers would ruin for her. She realized at that moment she would do anything to save what she had started with Jay. She would risk it all to be in his arms permanently.

"I want to taste you," he whispered as he kissed her neck. Instead of taking his time to kiss down her body, he lowered himself between her legs, gradually spreading them. When his tongue lapped at her clit, the passion radiated through the very core of her body.

"Oh Jay!" she moaned, running her hands thought his hair.

He ran his tongue over her folds before returning to her clit. The sensation was unlike anything she'd ever experienced. Her previous lovers weren't interested in her pleasure; it was just a mutual sex agreement. One that promised them no problems with her brothers, and she wouldn't have to deal with their guardian angels.

"Jay, please. I want you."

"In time, Sugar," he whispered before working his way up her body, taking time to pay attention to each of her nipples. He drew his tongue around each nipple before taking it into his mouth and sucking on it with such desire he had her moaning with pleasure.

She surrendered completely to his masterful seduction as he drained away all her doubts and fears.

He slowly slid his cock into her pussy as she cried out with need.

In and out slowly, he teased her sensitive flesh. Her body ached for release. She wanted him faster, but something inside of her said that if she mentioned it, he would only take longer.

As the passion began to mount, she dug her finger nails into his flesh, arching her back. She cried out in ecstasy. His control broke and he brought them both to the climax they needed. He drew her to a height of passion she never knew before, one that had her tingling under his fingertips and uncontrollable joy flooding through her.

He rolled off her, with his body closer to the door to protect her if the need arose. Their legs still intertwined, he wrapped his arms around her.

# Chapter Seven

Early the next morning they awoke to the bedside phone ringing. "Don't answer it," Jay said in a sleep-filled voice.

"It has to be important if they're disturbing us." She reached for the phone, knocking the base off the stand. She put the receiver to her ear as she pulled the receiver up.

"Yes?"

"Ms. Harper, this is Kathy. Your brother is insisting on speaking with you. Do you want me to put you through to him?"

She could see Jay shaking his head no, but he was still her brother. "Will he know where the call is coming from?"

"No, unless you tell him."

"Then put me through. I might as well get it over with." She wasn't happy about the early morning wakeup call and that wasn't going to work in Matthew's favor.

"Meg, is that you?"

"Yes, Matthew. What do you want? Do you realize how early it is?" The annoyance was already appearing in her voice.

"I want you to come to my room. We need to talk."

"You know, Matthew, I don't think there is much for us to say. You and Dan deceived me. You tracked me down like a lost dog. I'm a grown woman and it's about time you started treating me like one. I'm tired and want to enjoy the rest of my vacation."

"Meg, this isn't over. We need to discuss the fact that you are some lion's chew toy. Or have you become a full-blown sex toy?" His anger was growing, as was hers.

"Matthew, what I do or don't do and with who is none of your damn business!" she hollered at him before slamming the phone down on the cradle.

Jay rubbed his hand along her back. "Why do you let him do this to you?"

She wouldn't allow herself to cry. She was tired of how her brothers, especially Matthew, made her feel as if she couldn't control her own life. They always questioned her decisions, as though she wasn't smart enough to make an intelligent decision herself.

"I don't know. They've always done this to me."

"Have you ever thought that you needed to get away from your family?" he asked as she rolled back into his arms.

"I have. That's why I'm here. This vacation was supposed to give me time to myself. Time to get my thoughts together."

"No, Sugar. I meant move away from them."

She nodded. "I have, but without my family, I couldn't make it in the world. I have no control over my ability. The only reason I can hold down a job is because I'm a personal assistant to a vampire."

He snarled when she mentioned vampires. "I don't like the idea of you working with a vampire."

"It's my only option. Vampires don't have guardian angels looking for my help."

"I still don't like the idea, Sugar. You could get hurt."

She was touched by the fact that he cared, but she had to support herself. She couldn't be a burden on her family.

"Tell me why you hate vampires. What happened to your neck?" she asked as she ran her finger over his scar.

His body tensed as she traced the damage, triggering the memories of the event. He stared into thin air as if he were watching the events unfold again in front of his very eyes and there was nothing he could do to stop them. She could feel his body ripple with the anger he was feeling, his jaw set tight. She wanted to comfort him, to tell him she didn't need him to tell the story, but curiosity had the best of her.

"A few years ago, I was visiting a friend, Kate. She was dating a vampire. He was staying in her basement. I didn't have a problem with that for the same reason you don't seem concerned about vampires. I thought they could control themselves." He stared at the ceiling before continuing. "He tore Kate's throat out, and then came after me. I was asleep when it happened, but instantly awakened when his fangs entered my throat."

When he didn't continue, she asked, "What happened to the vampire?"

"Kate told me she placed a stake in the bedside table in case things got out of control. I thought at the time she meant in case I became uneasy with the vampire. But after she died, I found out she was worried he was starting to lose his mind. His desire for human blood was overtaking him, causing him not to think straight. She feared for her safety, but still stayed with him. She thought she loved him and that she would be enough to save him. Boy was she wrong." He paused, looking at her, and brushed a stray hair from her cheek. "If she would have told me, I could have saved her. She didn't deserve to die like that."

"I'm sorry." She leaned up to kiss his cheek, running her fingers up and down his arm in a comforting way.

"I shoved the stake right through his ribcage and into his heart. If I wasn't a shifter, I would have died just like Kate."

"It isn't your fault about your friend. When you love someone, you think you can save them."

"That's why I'm here. I am the alpha of my people; I need to be at my best at all times. Distractions put my people at risk. I can't have that. I told myself if I couldn't get it together during this week, then I would step down, hand the reins over to my second in command, Chase. I don't want that. I'm not one to take orders; I am a leader."

"Jay, you need to forgive yourself. There's nothing you could have done. When you entered the cabin with Sarah and Kathy, I could see your pain, and how bone tired you were. You deserve a chance to be happy. To do that, you must forgive yourself."

A soft smile was on his face as he touched her cheek. "You make me happy."

She wasn't sure what to say to that. Thankfully, she didn't have to; he kissed her. His soft velvet lips kissed her as though she was all he needed.

# Chapter Eight

"One, two, and three...now exhale," Bethany said as she led the yoga class. "That's enough for now. Please feel free to join in on one of the later classes or tomorrow."

As Meg and Jay started to leave, she saw Bethany motion for her.

"If you're not busy, I wanted to speak with you for a moment." She took a long swig from her water bottle.

"No, we were just going to go for a walk. We have time."

"Meg, I think I might have an idea to help you with your ability."

He cleared his throat. "I don't think you need me for this. I can come back later."

Before he could leave, Bethany caught him. "Actually, it would be helpful to her if you stayed. You might be able to share some tricks with her." Bethany turned her attention back to Meg. "You need to create a shield to protect yourself. Jay already does that, and if I'm correct, I believe he would be able to draw you into his shield. It would help you understand what you need to create for yourself."

"I can do that," he said, nodding to Bethany.

"Then show her. Do it and allow it to block my guardian angel from getting to her."

He nodded and looked down at Meg. "You have to trust me. This won't hurt, but the sensations might be bizarre."

"I trust you with my life. Let's do this. I'm willing to do anything that could help."

She watched him close his eyes and bring her body close to him. Moments later, little pin pricks surrounded her, not really hurting, but just letting her know something was amiss.

"Oh my! It's gone!" The excitement in her voice was obvious.

Keeping up his shield, he opened her eyes. "It's not hard. At first it will take concentration. I just focused my mind on protecting you. You need to think of the guardian angels as enemies you need to protect yourself from, that will help. With some practice, a shield will be second nature to you."

"Very good. I'm so glad it worked. Jay, drop your shield so she can try," Bethany said as she sat back down on the floor.

The moment the shield was dropped, the guardian angel was back. Bethany's angel didn't try to get her to change Bethany's faith, so she must be on the right track. Meg believed that Bethany's angel was her mother. She looked just like an older version of Bethany, the same brown hair, only cut shorter in a bob.

She tried to focus on protecting herself from the angel, tried to bring up the shield that would keep the guardian angels at bay. All she was able to do was make it appear behind a fog.

"Don't get frustrated. It takes practice," she said as she patted Meg's hand. "I see my next class coming. You are more than welcome to stay, but I think Jay might be able to help you with the shield."

# Chapter Nine

Instead of the walk they were both looking forward to, they went to the terrace, where they could enjoy the water views. They needed someone around for her to know her shield was working. Jay's angel was always there, as if it was a part of who he was.

In the garden, Jill Brady, Richard's wife, was tending the plants. "Welcome."

Jay led the way to a bench. "Do you mind if we sit awhile? Meg needs to work on her shielding abilities, and having another person around would be helpful so she could know her efforts are working."

"That's fine. Enjoy. Good luck," she said, returning to her work.

"Come on, Sugar. Focus. Picture the guardian angel pestering you to help them. Now bring up your shield."

She listened to what he said and each time her shield got stronger and stronger till she finally did it. She completely blocked Jill's guardian angel. She could still see Jay's angel through her shield, but it didn't bother her. Seeing even just one less guardian angel was a miracle.

"I did it," she said happily. For the first time, she felt blissfully happy and alive. Nothing would bring her down.

Then she saw Matthew walking towards them.

"I finally found you," he said as he approached.

"I know you want to fight with your sister, but now is not the time. She is developing a shield to help with her ability," Jay said, trying to hold off the confrontation that was sure to happen.

"I don't care what she is trying to do. We'll deal with this problem once and for all," he said, trying to sidestep Jay.

Jill looked up from her gardening as if she should call for security, and Jay whispered, "It's fine. We'll take it away from the other guests."

He placed a hand on the small of her back. "Let's go somewhere more private or they'll call Richard and security."

She nodded and followed him down the steps and away from the resort. When they were far enough away, she turned to Matthew. "Matthew, please. I really don't want to deal with you now. I am here for myself. I need to control my ability. You know what it does to me."

"You have dealt fine with your ability all these years. Don't use that as an excuse now."

"You call living alone, with no life, working for a vampire, controlling my ability? I don't!" she yelled at her brother. "I want to live. I want to have a family of my own. I don't want to be a burden on you and everyone else."

"You're not a burden, Meg. We love you."

"You love me! Is that why you never told me the truth about what happened to Mom or Jonathon? All those years you made me believe she died in childbirth." She could see Matthew giving Jay a look of hatred. "Don't you dare blame him! He's the first person who cared enough to tell me the truth."

"The truth? And what does the little furball consider the truth?"

"He told me what the alpha's orders were. Mom was supposed to go home to her people, but she refused. She didn't want to leave us behind. The alpha ordered her to be returned; instead, she was killed. But that has nothing to do with Jay or his people. The blood lies on the alpha's hands, not on the shifters."

"Mom's blood is on the shifters' hands, all shifters." She could tell he was angry, and ready to strike out. His temper, when crossed, could be uncontrollable.

"Matthew, don't do this. The only ones who deserve the blame are the ones who attacked that night. Jay was a child when the attack happened; he is not to blame."

His eyes conveyed the fury that made her wonder if her brother would lose control. "Did he tell you his father was among the animals that night?"

She could feel Jay go still behind her, and a pain shot through her heart. She turned to look at him briefly, a look of confusion on her face. Finding out that Jay's father was involved from her brother made everything worse.

Jay still had his arm around her as he leaned down to whisper in her ear. "I think it might be best if we finish this discussion in the room."

She eyed him doubtfully. She wasn't sure taking Matthew back to their cabin was a wise move.

"Meg, I think it would be better than having everyone overhear what we're talking about. I don't think you want your family business aired in public."

She nodded, not entirely convinced this was the right thing.

"Matthew, let's go to Meg's cabin and I can explain. I think Meg would prefer if everyone didn't know your family business."

# Chapter Ten

In the cabin, Jay started a fire while she spoke quietly to Matthew. She was sure Jay could hear everything she said to Matthew, but she didn't care. "Matthew, you are my brother and I love you, but I won't stand for you interfering with my life any longer. I don't know where things are going with Jay, but I want the chance to explore them. If you can't accept it or what he is, then I don't want to be around you. I let you live your own life; and I expect the same in return."

Her brother stood there silently with his muscular arms crossed over his chest. He looked as if he was a bouncer in a club, not having a conversation with his sister at a resort.

Out of the corner of her eye, she could see Jay standing silently by the fireplace, waiting for them to finish. This was like talking to the brick wall. She didn't know why she even tried. Someday she would learn. She took the first step, and instead of trying to talk some sense into Matthew, she took a deep breath and then exhaled. She turned and walked away from him; heading straight into Jay's waiting arms.

Sinking into the safety of his arms, she saw Matthew grind his teeth with fury, but she didn't care. She loved him, but this fit he threw every time she tried to live her own life was getting ridiculous.

"Matthew, come join us and let's discuss this like reasonable adults," she said as watched him.

"I'm fine where I am." He didn't move, as if he was afraid.

She wanted to tell him what a jerk he was being, but she held her tongue. Jay gave her arm a light squeeze. "Let's just get this over with." She suddenly felt weary of the whole thing.

"Yes, my father was a part of the team that came that night," Jay started, but before he could finish, Matthew cut him off.

"See what I mean? You are standing next to the son of the man who helped kill our mother!" he screamed.

She didn't give in to Matthew's temper; instead she placed her hand in Jay's to let him know that he had her support.

"If you would let me finish," he said to Matthew. "My father came on the mission to make sure your mother was returned unharmed. The alpha sent some of his most aggressive guards after your mother when she disobeyed his order. My father was there because he didn't want anything to happen to her. My father fought the alpha over this decision. He thought taking her away from her children was the wrong move."

"You believe this shit?" Matthew asked.

"Yes, I do. You know I can tell when someone is lying to me. Their guardian angel gives them away. Jay isn't lying. He has no reason to lie to us. Unlike you and the rest of the family. All those years I didn't pay attention to what was right before my eyes. I brushed off the hits I was receiving from all the guardian angels in the family, because I figured it was something small about Mom. I thought I was only getting the impression you and everyone else were lying to me because you blamed me for Mom's death."

"It wasn't long after that mission that my people overturned the alpha and gained control. They were tired of being used." He must have noticed Matthew rolling his eyes, as he was famous in the family for doing, because he added, "Matthew, I'm sorry for what happened that night. My father tried to stop it, but he was too late. The mission was moved up and he wasn't told about the time change. He believed they realized his plans and went without him. When he got there, it was already too late."

"Whatever lets you sleep at night, buddy." Matthew retorted in anger.

"Matthew, do you realize you are acting like a child? When are you going to grow up? All this anger is making you a very bitter person. I can't take it anymore," Meg told him sadly, trying to hold back the tears that wanted to burst free.

"Then don't deal with it. It looks as though you're pretty friendly with the enemy. Why don't you just move into the enemy camp?" he hollered at her, oblivious to the fact he was breaking her heart.

"I will not have you treat your sister like this in my presence. She deserves better than this."

"Who the hell do you think you are? This is a family matter and I think you need to leave," Matthew said, pushing off the wall and coming to stand in front of Jay, spoiling for a fight.

She knew she had to get this situation under control soon or there would be nothing she could do. "Matthew, Jay has been better to me in the last few days then you have ever been. You should be happy I found someone that treats me right, not like how you treat me. If you can't respect me, my feelings, or my guests, then it is time you make your exit."

"Meg, you don't know what you're saying. He brainwashed you or something," he said, realizing that his sister was serious.

"No one brainwashed me, Matthew. It's just the first time I've spoken up for myself, and you know what? It feels pretty good. I won't have you and the rest of the family treating me like you have always done; when we return home, things will change."

"If you stay here with him, then don't bother coming home," he said as he strolled to the door.

"My dear brother, you don't know how happy those words make me. I would rather be on my own than return home to the box you try to keep me in."

He slammed the door, marking his exit, and instead of feeling sad over the loss of her family, she felt alive. She wanted a life and now she had it, even if it meant starting over somewhere else. She had all she really needed here in her suitcase. When she left the resort, she could go anywhere.

# Chapter Eleven

Later that evening as they lay in bed, talking, Jay turned to her. "Were you serious?"

"About what?" she asked in a sleepy voice.

"About not returning to your family?"

"Yes. I'm not sure where I'm going yet, but I need a fresh start. I can't go back to the way things were." She thought about it off and on all day, but she didn't know where she wanted to go. She didn't want her vacation to end, because that meant her time with Jay would end as well.

He rolled to face her, the moonlight providing enough light for them to see each other clearly. "Meg, I have given this a lot of thought. I love you. I don't want this to end; I want to be with you. Come home to Maine with me."

"Oh Jay!" Her heart sang with delight. "I love you, too. Yes. Wherever you are, I want to be there with you."

"You might regret that when you meet my sisters," he said, his voice full of joy and happiness.

She kissed him, as her emotions whirled and skidded out of control.

"There is one more thing," he said before kissing her again. "I don't want to have to fight off anyone else. I want you all to myself. Will you marry me?"

She was caught off guard, but her heart sung the answer. "Yes. I love you, Jay Wilder."

She kissed him, knowing this time their desire would take over. Knowing there would be no more discussion, or wedding plans, at least until the morning. Tonight they would explore each other for the first time not as lovers, but as mates.

# Learning What Love Is

Jacey Wilder is always watching over her shoulder, worried her abusive ex will find her. Terrifyingly, her natural strength as a lioness shifter proves no match against him. When her brother suggests a vacation to Half Moon Harbor Resort—a resort that caters to the paranormal—she leaps at the chance to get away.

Self-defense expert Blake Blackwell's lion paced within him demanding they claim their newly discovered mate. The last self-defense class he had to teach at the Half Moon Harbor Resort was all that stood in his way. Or did it?

Can Jacey accept Blake as her destined mate or will her ex destroy her potential happiness? Blake lost one woman he loved but he'll be damned if he loses Jacey.

# Chapter One

Jacey Wilder held the cell phone in a death grip. Anger had her animal crawling to the surface. She kicked herself for her stupidity over Gray. Would she never learn? Why was she so set on changing him, when it was obvious he didn't want to—and would never change?

The family fixer, she solved her family's problems. Gray, a true bad boy on the wrong path, allured her with his overwhelming issues in need of the "right" woman to make it better. The man took everyone for granted, and she wanted to help him turn his life around. Falling for him hadn't been in the cards.

"Jacey, it's about time you gave up on that dirtbag," Jackie said from where she relaxed on the porch swing.

"Were you listening in on my phone call again?" She eyed her twin with suspicion.

"I couldn't help it, your anger was so strong I could feel it out here. I wanted to know what happened this time." Jackie moved her legs to give Jacey room to sit down. "Are you really done this time? Before you get all defensive, I'm just asking because we've heard this before."

"Yes, Jackie. *I am done.* It's time for me to move on," The tears in her voice angered her. She was tired of being used by Gray, yet her emotions were out of control when it came to him. A car door closed and she looked away from her sister.

*Oh, Blake.* The glimpse of her sexy new neighbor, his scent called to her inner lioness, and made both stand up and take notice. The sight of him was one of the perks of her day. Blake Blackwell was one of the few in their town who wasn't a part of the Wilder family or somehow related. Blake's grandmother had remarried a distant cousin of a Wilder mate. When she died, he'd inherited her house and bookstore.

Jackie scooted closer and put her arm around Jacey "I know it's not easy but you deserve better. What I'm about to say next is because I love you, so please remember that when you want to strangle me."

"What is it?" she prodded when her sister paused.

"Here it goes…Jay and his new bride, Meg, will be here shortly."

"I can't believe you waited until now to tell me. You know Jay's going to flip if he sees me upset over Gray again." She rushed into the house to repair her makeup. Her stomach had butterflies at the thought of Jay and Meg finally being back home. Jay had been away for too long, it would be nice to have him back among the Wilder Pride.

In the downstairs bathroom, she took a washrag to the mascara running down her cheeks. Jackie yelled "They're here," and her time was up. She tossed the rag in the sink, and then she looked in the mirror. A quick fluff of her blonde, curly hair would have to do. She didn't have time to redo her makeup.

Her puffy, red-rimmed eyes made her crying apparent. "Hopefully Meg has tamed the lion," she told her reflection and went to greet her brother and new sister-in-law.

Jay, their once lost brother, waited with Jackie and his mate on the porch. After his vampire attack, he hadn't been the same. Since taking over command of the Wilder Pride, her brother was always tense. In the last few months, the situation worsened. He was quicker to anger, his temper always boiling slightly under the surface. Thankfully, his new mate restored the spark in Jay's eyes. Meg was one of the few in Wilderville who wasn't a lion shifter, but Jackie knew she would fit in. Her ability to see a person's guardian angels made it difficult to live a normal life. Around shifters she would find the peace she craved, since they didn't have guardian angels demanding her help like the average human.

"There's my other favorite sister. Nice of you to be here to welcome me home," he teased. "Jacey, come meet Meg, my beautiful mate and wife." Her brother jumped off the porch to dig their luggage out of the trunk.

Meg's nerves mingled with Jacey's anger, making her giddy and on edge. "Welcome to the family." Jacey gave her a hug and leapt down to follow him.

Jay grabbed the last suitcase out of the trunk before turning towards Jacey. "Meg, Jacey's going to help me take the bags to the house, I'll be back in a minute." He nodded his head towards the direction of his house across the street. "Then we'll all go out for dinner and catch up."

*Shit. Impossible to hide things from him, I should have snuck out the back door.* Left with no choice she picked up the smaller bag from the pavement, and followed him across the street. Delaying would put off the inevitable.

Shifters possessed the uncanny ability to feel the emotions of others, especially those closest to them. Jay as the alpha of Wilderville had honed his ability to seek out traitors amongst his people. He dropped the suitcases by the foot of the stairs and rounded on her. "What's going on? Spill it and don't tell me nothing I can feel the turmoil. Is it Gray again?"

Suddenly the bag weighed a hundred pounds. She opened her fingers and it fell to the floor. Tugging at her sweater, she wished she could wrap herself in it and disappear as she did when they were cubs. For years Jay had been there with her through thick and thin. It wasn't until he saw the bruises that he pushed for her to leave Gray.

"It's nothing. I'm just tired." She tried to diffuse his concern.

"Don't give me that bullshit. I know you better than that Jacey. The only thing you get this upset about is Gray. I thought you weren't seeing him anymore."

She plopped down on the steps. She fiddled with a loose string on her red sweater unable to make eye contact. "I haven't seen him since before you left."

When she didn't continue, he knelt in front of her. "Jacey, tell me what's going on. Either you're lying or…"

"No matter how many times I tell him that it's over, he calls me daily. He won't come here because he knows Chase or one of the others will kill him on your orders. But he stopped by work so much that I got fired. I'm scared to leave Wilderville, but staying here with him calling me constantly I can't get over him. I don't know what to do." The dam burst and she poured out her pain and anger. She twirled the string around her fingers unable to look her brother in the eye. These were the times Jay was just her brother not her alpha. She wanted his support, and guidance without the pride knowing. But as alpha Jay would bring in the Wilderville guards to deal with the situation.

Jay placed his hand on hers. "I'll deal with him. We will go to the police if we have to. This harassment needs to end, you should have told me before."

"You were away at Half Moon Harbor, then your honeymoon. There hasn't been time, plus I was trying to deal with him myself. I thought I was handling it, at least the best I could. Without work, I barely leave Wilderville. I did my best to avoid his calls, but today he caught me."

"We'll take care of it." He repeated firmly. "Maybe a break from around here would be good for you. Half Moon Harbor has excellent security; they also cater to our kind. We could arrange for you to have a private cabin there. It would give you the time you need to get your emotions in order, and time to heal. There's no cell phone service so he won't be able to contact you."

She nodded maybe it was just what she needed. She could get to know Meg when she returned. A few days not having to dodge the phone, or being cramped in her house sounded like heaven. *I pushed Jay to go to Half Moon Harbor Resort. It helped him. Jay always wanted to protect us, now I'm giving him the chance and he's jumping at it.* She embraced his offer with open arms, dying to get away from Wilderville. After all, she was the one who found Half Moon Harbor Resorts for Jay when she thought he needed a break.

# Chapter Two

"Kevin's going as your guard. He'll keep his distance, but will be there if you need him. Half Moon Harbor has good security but I want one of ours with you as a precaution. Don't fight me on this, Jacey. I'm not taking any chances." Jay put her suitcase in the trunk.

Jacey let out a heavy sigh. Getting out of Wilderville was what she wanted but having a guard was an unexpected negative. "Jay…"

"Don't argue with me. It's for your protection. Kevin's a good guard, and better yet he knows how to keep watch from a distance. He won't be in your way. It's either he goes or you stay."

"I'm a grown woman, I can protect myself." She wanted to believe those words but Gray had proved more than once her lioness was no match to his strength.

"Listen to him Jacey. You're not going by yourself." Jackie leaned against the car waiting for her chance to say goodbye. She has the distinct feeling she was back in school again, except back then, she and her sister ganged up on Jay. Two against one wasn't fair. She wanted to roll her eyes, which she hadn't done in years. All through school Jay protected her when someone teased her. The other kids thought she was weird, but in truth, she had a hard time suppressing her animal.

Her inability to suppress her lioness around humans as a child inspired the Wilder Pride to buy up the surrounding area. Wilderville was a safe haven for their pride of lion shifters. They even provided a small school for not only the Wilderville children to go but for all shifter children if they desired. Wilderville School was a designated safe zone, protected by joint treaty. Anyone caught fighting amongst their own kind or others would be removed. The policy extended to include the staff and parents as well as the children. It was just another way that the Wilder children—especially Jay, Jackie, and Jacey—played a part in keeping the shifters' secret.

The other Wilder children were only part time residents of Wilderville, and had their own lives beyond its safe haven. Jacey and her siblings devoted their attention to the Wilderville community—Jay more than any of them as the alpha of their pride.

"He's going, end of story. Now get in the car. We'll pick him up on the way." Jay dismissed her and turned to kiss his wife. His voice softened, love and desire gentling his tone. "I'll be back soon."

Jacey huffed a sigh, but obeyed. She took one last look around. She never went farther than a few hours' drive from Wilderville, and here she was about to get on a plane to Half Moon Harbor Resort. It was a little overwhelming.

* * *

As the ferry—the last part of her journey to the island—made its way across the ocean towards Half Moon Harbor, Jacey's cell phone beeped. Her cell service didn't extend this far. Liberation flooded through her veins. She had made it without a single call from Gray. She pulled her phone out of her pocket, and sighed with appreciation at the sight of no signal.

*I made it.* The horizon peeled back, revealing her destination. The golden sands sparkled, against the greens of the thick forest they reserved for shifters to roam free. She wasn't sure what she would do with a whole week to herself, but she knew she needed it, just as she knew she needed the air she breathed. The trip gave her time to think. It had opened her eyes to the fact she couldn't keep living sheltered inside Wilderville, concerned to answer her phone for fear it was Gray on the other end. Having Kevin tag along was an unexpected bump, but she wouldn't let it ruin her break.

As if summoned by her thoughts, Kevin approached with their suitcases in tow. His skin seemed pale, and he looked terrified. His white cowboy hat sat low on his head, if they had been the same height she wouldn't have been able to see his eyes. The hat and boots were the only thing that distinguished him as not an original Wilderville pride member. When the ferry came to a halt at the dock, he looked relieved. "Can we get off of this moving death trap now?"

*Who would have guessed the man of steel was petrified of being on the water?* Strong Kevin could take down a bear with his own two hands and a ferryboat ride scared him. Why Jay chose a hydrophobic Kevin as her escort when he should have been able to sense his lieutenant's fear of the water she didn't know.

She nodded. "Not much for boats, are you?"

"That obvious?" He stayed close to her side as they made their way from the dock. When their feet hit solid land, she could have sworn she heard him sigh with gratitude. "When I was a kid my mom had a gentlemen friend with a boat. They got this crazy idea we should take a trip. Turned out he wasn't much of a sailor…a nasty storm came and the boat capsized—he went down with the ship. My mom and I were on a life raft for two days before the coast guard found us. I've been terrified of the water since."

"Wow. I can't believe you came with me then."

"Jay can be pretty convincing. You can't blame him for wanting you protected." Kevin moved them out of the way to allow the people boarding the ferry access. "Remember that…"

A man walked up to them and Kevin went silent and stepped forward, putting himself in front of her. His shoulder length black hair was tied in at the nap of his neck, his sea green eyes sparkled as the sun hit them. "Miss Wilder, I'm Richard Brady, the head of security for the resort." He held his hand out to her. "You're brother has made us aware of your situation. We have ensured him you'll be safe here. I've come to escort you to your cabin, and to let you know that if you have any concerns please contact me immediately."

She took his hand, all the while cursing her brother. Jay—the protector—would shelter her and her sisters if they would let him. "Thank you Mr. Brady, but I don't expect to have any problems. I also have Kevin here."

He nodded. "Richard, please. With the weather turning chilly, we only have a few guests. You'll have plenty of privacy. We have put you in cabin five and Kevin's in cabin four, right next door." He reached down and picked up her bright pink suitcase. "If you'll follow me."

The brick path to the cabins from the dock was lined with colorful flowers, and the slight incline added to the spectacular views. She was glad she remembered to pack her canvas and paints. Maybe with Gray out of the picture she could reclaim the things she loved again.

"Kevin, that's your cabin there, but I assume you wish to inspect Miss Wilder's before you settle in." Richard nodded to the small cabin before continuing another few feet up the path. "This is it."

Richard led the way to the door, with Jacey and Kevin in tow. While being here away from it all revived her, she couldn't wait to be settled and be alone. Richard unlocked the door, and stepped aside allowing them to enter.

The cabin was done in warm tones, offering the feel of home. The walls were a deep shade of brown. A large caramel shaded sectional dominated the sitting area, in front of the fireplace, and cream-colored throws draped each corner. A large bay window provided an excellent view of the beach below and the waves crashing onto the shore.

"The bedroom is through that door." Richard said setting her suitcase down. "Dinner is served in the dining hall at six o'clock. There's room service for breakfast and lunch. I'll check back with you later, but if you need anything I'm around." He placed two sets of keys—one for her and the other for Kevin—on the small entry table by the door before he left.

"Thank you." Jacey gave him a quick smile.

"I'll check the bedroom." Kevin leaned down and grabbed her suitcase before moving towards the door Richard pointed out.

She watched him leave and sank into the plush cushions of the couch. The foamy waves beat at the beach below. She had a fleeing thought of taking a stroll on the beach, as the sun sank into the ocean, but she pushed it off until tomorrow. She was just too tired.

"Everything's secure. Do you want me to stay for a bit?" She didn't hear Kevin until she felt his presence behind her.

"I'm fine, just tired. I might take a nap before dinner."

He gave her shoulder a gentle rub. "Okay. I'll be back shortly before six and we can go to dinner together." Before she could tell him she could make it to the dining hall by herself he was gone.

She laid there thinking about Kevin. He was a good man, too bad he was in love with Jackie. In Kevin's eyes, she could never compare to her twin. They might be identical, but they were completely different people. Jackie, a teacher at the Wilderville School was the outgoing popular one. A romantic at heart, Jacey preferred the quiet and wanted a lover to sweep her off her feet. She thought she found that with Gray but it was just a facade.

Jacey never understood why Jackie pretended to be blind to how devoted Kevin was to her. He was head over heels in love with Jackie. Even more mystifying was why he hadn't stepped forward and made his claim. Even she could smell the mating scent on them.

Jacey would give anything to have someone look at her the way Kevin looked at her sister.

The thought of romance had her reaching into her carry-on bag for her favorite romance novel. Her fingers gripped the worn paperback. The beloved book was dog-eared and tattered from many hours of enjoyment. Even as the pages became loose and threatened to fall out she cherished the copy. She read this book so often that she practically knew it word for word. If she closed her eyes she could have the scenes play out before her.

She brought it to her chest, her fingers brushed over the faded cover. Maybe reading romance novels gave her an unrealistic view of men. She wanted her own hero, just like the ones in all her novels.

# Chapter Three

Kevin strolled through the reception area, the cool air a relief against his heated skin. The short walk from the cabins left him craving a cold drink. First he needed to call Jay and let him know they had arrived safely.

"Kevin." Richard stepped out of the office to the right of the reception desk. "Everything suitable in the cabins?"

He gave Richard halfhearted smile. Something about him bugged Kevin. The predatory look in his eyes when he greeted Jacey and the proprietary air when he escorted them to their cabins. He saw Jacey as someone to claim and she deserved better. There was no way that Richard would sink his claws into Jacey on his watch. "Yeah. The cabins are fine. Jacey's settled in. I need to make a call…let her brother know she's here safely."

"You can use my office. I have something to take care of anyway." Richard shifted his bulky frame to the side, giving Kevin a straight shot to the office.

He let out a low growl. "Jacey's napping. Leave *her* alone."

To Richard's credit, he didn't even deny his attraction to Jacey. "What is it to you? She's not your mate, nor has she been claimed. She's fair game."

"Leave her alone. That's the only warning you will get. She deserves better than a horny wolf." His relationship with Jacey might be as platonic as they came, but he'd be damned if he'd let someone hurt her again. She had already been through too much with Gray.

* * *

Jacey picked at her food. The dining hall was half-empty. The other guests went about their business—to pursue their evening activities. Never a social butterfly, she possessed even less desire to be around others.

"Jacey, what's wrong?" Kevin, her ever-watchful guardian, drank his coffee while she nibbled on her dinner with no enthusiasm.

She laid her fork aside, and met his gaze. "I have this nagging feeling something's going to happen. I can't explain it, I just know something's wrong. Sometimes I can sense things. I think coming here was a bad idea. I need to go home."

"You're safer here."

"I'm not worried about me. Gray…"

Kevin laid his hand over hers, cutting her off before she could voice her concern about Gray. The warmth of his touch was fire against her cool skin. "Gray isn't here. You're safe. Jay and Chase will take care of him. You'll see you can move on with your life."

"He'll hurt them." She whispered barely able to find her voice.

"I promise you they'll be fine. They can take care of themselves. You need to focus on you for once." He gave her hand a gentle squeeze. "If you're not going to eat that, let's go. It's a nice night for a walk."

She took a final sip of her coffee and conceded. "Just a short walk." She agreed out of guilt, not any real desire to stretch her legs. Kevin was here because of her. The least she could do was be suitable company.

The breeze coming off the water tousled her hair. They made their way down the path. Their steps fell into sync and they moved away from the few guest still gathered in the garden area. "Kevin, can I ask you something?"

"Sure." He slipped his cowboy hat back on now that they were outside.

"Why haven't you claimed Jackie? I know you're her mate."

He drew her off the path to a small sitting area. He stood there staring down at the glistening water below and her hope he'd answer faded.

After a long silence, he sighed. "Jackie deserves more. We have many differences. She flourishes in a crowd, where I prefer the quiet. My position in the pride makes it difficult to have relationships with those under me."

"You'd rather deny not only yourself, but also Jackie the chance of finding happiness with their mate?" Why would anyone deny what was something that was theirs? She couldn't understand the concept.

"What does it matter...Jackie doesn't even know I exist."

"That's where you're wrong. She might not admit it but she knows you're her mate. Pa was old fashion and we were raised with his beliefs. Women don't pursue men. She'll idly sit by waiting for you forever. Jackie deserves happiness and you can give it to her. Everything else will fall into place or you two wouldn't have been destined to be mates. Think about it." She wanted to shake him. He was giving up something she couldn't only hope to find someday. Guilt racked her for betraying her sister, but she wanted to see them happy. One of them should be. "I'm turning in. I'll see you in the morning."

The short walk to the cabin only served to make her restless. Instead of entering the cabin she walked around the side of it to a path down to the beach below that she noticed earlier. With each step, her anger flowed through her. What a cruel world it was that Kevin and Jackie had something she had wanted for so long, yet neither of them pursued it.

# Chapter Four

Jacey slipped off her shoes, tossed them at the foot of the path and stepped onto the cool sand. She always loved the beach, and how the sand felt under her feet. To make the most of it she curled her toes. The soft, little granulates gritted between her toes.

With a quick glance around to make sure she was alone on the beach, she made her way to the water. The air became cooled and she wished she'd brought a sweater, but her three quarter length sleeve shirt would have to do.

She made it to the water line in time to splash in a wave lapping onto the shore. The surprisingly warm water rushed around her ankles. She basked in the moonlight lost in her thoughts.

"Jacey?" A low voice called from behind her.

Fear flooded through her body. Her heart pounded in her ears, and threatened to beat right out of her chest. She dug deep to find whatever courage she could before she turned around. "Blake?" His shaggy brown hair, jawline stubble, and deep green eyes were unmistakable even in the subdued light from the moon. The man who frequented her dreams stood before her just as she pictured him.

His bare chest called to her. How she wanted to feel him. *This is not the time. I can't fantasize about naked men until I've dealt with Gray.*

"I'm sorry. I didn't mean to scare you. I was out for a walk and I thought that was you."

She did her best to calm her erratic heartbeat. She didn't fear him. "It's okay. I thought I was alone. What are you doing here?"

"I used to work here before I moved to Wilderville. I was scheduled to teach one last class today. But I didn't expect to find you here."

"It was a last minute trip. I just needed to get away for a bit." She shoved her hands into the pocket of her jean shorts to try to hide her nerves. Her heart leapt to discover him here. Would being here at the same time provide an escape for them to explore each other without the pressures and complications of home?

"Half Moon Harbor is a great place to get away from it. It's what drew me back time after time." He lifted a red and black plaid blanket. "It's such a nice night. I thought I'd enjoy it. Care to join me?" He didn't wait for her answer, instead retreating to the dry sand. He laid out the blanket and sat down.

She came down here for privacy but against her better judgment she threw caution to the wind and made her way to him. "What do you teach?" She lowered herself to sit next to him.

He leaned back on one arm and she had to turn to see him better. "I teach self-defense."

The answer was simple yet she sensed there was more to the story. His voice held a hint of sorrow. "It must be hard to keep your lion in check for something like that."

"To save even one person it's worth it."

His words caught her off guard and left her unsure what to say next. They sat in uncomfortable silence as the waves pounded the shore. "Who did you lose?" Unable to contain the question, she held her breath for his answer. She sensed his loss was the reason for his interest in self-defense.

He collapsed back onto the blanket, his eyes closed. "My sister...she was in an abusive relationship and the asshole killed her a few years ago in a drunken rage."

The pain in his words rocked her. For years she had stayed with Gray all the while she denied his nature. With each bruise, she excused his actions, lied and covered for him. Gray fought with his fists as others spared with words. The last time he raised his hand to her he took it too far. She couldn't hide it from Jay and her family any longer, they forced her to open her eyes to the years of abuse.

"Jacey, you okay? You're shaking. Are you cold?" Blake rubbed her arm as if trying to chase the goosebumps away.

His touch sent fire through her veins. It took everything she had not to move closer into his embrace. *What's wrong with me? I can't get involved with someone now.* "Yeah." Her voice cracked and she had to swallow the lump in her throat. "I'm fine."

"That was inconsiderate of me...I wasn't thinking."

"It's fine." The fact he knew about her relationship with Gray flooded her with embarrassment. She pulled her legs into her chest, and held onto them with all her might. Maybe the beach would open up and swallow her whole. His knowledge shouldn't surprise her— Wilderville was a close-knit community. Even to someone who just joined the pride, their secrets and gossip would be known. "I should be going." Loathe to see pity in his eyes, she jumped to her feet. How could she forget her own weakness when it chased her everywhere?

"Jacey…" he rose to stand beside her. He reached out as if to touch her but pulled back. How she longed for his touch, even a brief one. "I have some loose ends to tie up in the morning, but will you meet me here tomorrow night? Same time."

"I don't know." She wanted to tell him yes, but stopped. Since he moved to Wilderville, she watched for him to come home with the hope of catching a quick glance of him. The brief sight of him each day gave her reason to hope for a future after Gray. It made her feel like a stalker but every free thought she had turned to him. She longed to run her hands over his chest, to feel the muscles that lay just beneath the skin.

# Chapter Five

"Where were you?" Kevin's voice came out of the shadows to her left and she jerked around. Too preoccupied she hadn't noticed him lurking—a flaw she seemed to experience far too much lately.

Kevin sat in a chair on the far corner of the dark deck. "Shit, Kevin you scared me." She opened the door to the cabin and reached in to the turn on the light switch in the living room. "What are you doing here?"

"You didn't answer my question." He stood stretching out his long legs.

"I went for a walk on the beach. I didn't know I was confined to my cabin."

"Confined…well let's just say you shouldn't be off wandering around without me knowing where you are. I'm here to keep you safe. Think of me as your bodyguard. I shouldn't have let you walk off alone. Your questions threw me. It won't happen again." He confronted her, a stern glare in his eyes. As threatening as he might look to other she knew he wouldn't harm her. Kevin was one of Jay's trusted guards, and could be provoked in a moment's notice, but Jay would kill him if he harmed a hair on her head.

She rolled her eyes at him. *I don't want a damn bodyguard.* "Do you want to come in? It's chilly out here. I'm sure in the fine print Jay added that I'm not to get sick while under your supervision." Kevin wasn't amused by the sarcasm in her voice but she didn't care. She wasn't sure getting out of Wilderville did as much as she hoped since instead of being confined at home, she would be under his constant supervision.

"That's okay. I just wanted to check on you before turning in. I shouldn't have left you to walk back to the cabin by yourself." He pivoted to leave, but she stepped into his path.

"Either this place is safe or it isn't. Jay said the security was the best here. I thought I was safe here. Do you know something I don't?" He avoided her gaze, but she wasn't having that. "What's going on Kevin?"

"Gray's brother was killed yesterday when he was caught in Wilderville." Her breath escaped her with a loud whooshing, as if all the air was deflating from her. If Kevin hadn't been standing next to her she would have collapsed onto the cold wood of the deck. He lifted her into his arms when her legs gave way and carried her inside.

*He'll kill Jay for this before coming after me. I should have never left him.* "I have to go home. If I go back to him maybe…"

He sat her on the couch, and knelt beside her. "Stop it Jacey. You're not going back to him. Let Jay and Chase deal with him, and while we're at it don't fight me when it comes to your protection. It's doubtful anyone is here that has connections to Gray but in case…"

\* \* \*

Blake pushed open the door to his small hotel room, mentally kicking himself for telling Jacey about his sister. Just days ago when he was with Chase—the second in command of the Wilderville pride—he received a call from Gray demanding that they returned Jacey to him.

Jacey didn't need him to shove her past in her face. She had her own bruises to heal. He needed to show her she deserved better. No man had the right to lay hands on a woman in the way Gray did. His anger vibrated through him seeking a release he couldn't find.

He paced the short walkway in front of the bed, the pale brown walls closed in around him. His lion paced within him, demanding he shift and go for a run. He was still considered a member of the staff and that was against the rules while guests were on the premises. Instead he'd have to make do in another way—a cold shower.

The anger at himself didn't dissipate the desire he held for Jacey. His shaft stood at attention, longing for Jacey—his mate.

# Chapter Six

The day dragged on as Jacey counted down the hours until her "date" with Blake on the beach. She busied herself playing cards with Kevin, but her gaze kept tracking to the clock.

"Why do you keep checking the time?" he asked tossing a card down.

"I'm not." She diverted her gaze with the hope he wouldn't sense she was lying before she picked up her card.

"You've always been a bad liar Jacey." He stared at her. "I know trusting is hard for you—especially after everything you've been through—but you can trust me."

"Did you know Blake was going to be here?" She sat her cards aside, and picked up her glass of ice tea. She took a sip and watched him.

"No." He too sat his cards aside, his forehead creasing with concern. "You've seen him?"

"Yeah. Last night he was on the beach." She pushed at a stray curl of hair, and tucked it behind her ear. "I'm meeting him again tonight."

"The hell you are," he roared at her. Years of dealing with Jay roaring at her and Jackie for one thing or another hadn't prepared her for Kevin's. Her shoulders sank, she wished she would have stuck with her initial plan and not told him.

"He's not a threat to me. He's part of the Wilderville pride." She hated feeling like a child who didn't know any better.

"You know nothing about him. He's new to our pride. With the current situation, until we know more about him you cannot see him. Jacey. Think about this. Doesn't it seem suspicious that he's here?"

She stood, and paced to the window. The setting sun cast pink and purple streaks through the sky. "Don't do this, Kevin." She refused to believe Blake had anything to do with Gray.

"What do you really know about him?"

"He lives next door to me. I know Jay wouldn't have let him come to Wilderville if he posed a threat to any of us. Jay's our alpha, he would have sensed if Blake was a traitor or if he was a threat."

"If he means no harm he'll understand and will wait until you're both back in Wilderville to see each other. I don't like the timing. If Chase or Jay knew he'd be here they'd have said." Kevin still sat at the table where they had been playing cards, but she could feel his gaze.

She ran her hand through her hair, and fought to gain rational perspective over the situation. She could see Kevin's worry, after all Jay had entrusted her safety to him, but she wouldn't let his concerns stop her from seeing Blake.

"He worked here. He had a commitment here, that's why he's here. I know Blake has nothing to do with Gray...his sister was killed by in an abusive relationship. He teaches self-defense here to try to save people from the fate his sister met. I'm going to see him tonight. I can't just leave him waiting down there waiting for me."

"I'll go." He rose and moved to the refrigerator.

"No. I'm going to see him." But she could be magnanimous. "You can come with me. If there is any problem we'll leave, and I won't fight you on not seeing him again while we're here."

He finished pouring more tea into his glass and looked at her, disapproval etched into his expression. It was clear he wasn't happy with the idea.

"Either agree to it, or I'll go without you. Even if I have to wait until the middle of the night to get away from you."

"You're a stubborn woman." He leaned against the counter, his arms crossed over his chest.

She shot him a coy smile. "You better get used to it if you're going to claim Jackie."

\* \* \*

Jacey made her way across the sand to where Blake stood near the water's edge. Her stomach did summersaults. *Could he be here on Gray's orders? No, if Gray knew where I'd be he would have come himself.*

Blake turned away from the water to look at her and raised an eyebrow at the sight of Kevin a step behind her. "What's he doing here?"

"Can we sit? I'll explain everything." She nodded to the blanket he already had laid out. Kevin kept his distance as they had already agreed.

"Umm, sure." They made their way to the blanket in silence.

"Blake…" She looked down at her hands, her nerves getting the better of her.

"What's going on?" He set his hand over hers. From the corner of her eye, she could see Kevin's tensed posture.

"I know you've heard the stories…about Gray." Thankfully, he nodded and spared her further explanation. "I came here to get away from it all…from him. Jay wanted me somewhere safe, while he took care of the situation. Kevin's here as my bodyguard."

"He's worried I'll harm you." Blake said cutting straight to the point.

"You don't know Jay's temper. If I so much as get a paper cut…well you get the point."

"Let's put his fears to rest. Your cabin or the dining room should be empty now we can use it. We'll sit down and I'll do my best to eliminate his concerns." He rose, and pulled her with him.

"My cabin will give us more privacy." She brushed the butt of her shorts off. "You don't have to do this."

"I suspect if I want to see you *alone* I have to." He gave her a wink.

* * *

Jacey sat next to Blake all the while Kevin hovered. She hated the feeling of him looming over her, but she tried to ignore it. She just wanted this over as quickly as possible. If Kevin wanted to stand she'd let him. He wanted it clear to Blake that his rank was higher.

"What are you doing here, Blake?" One thing Jacey normally liked about Kevin was he wasn't one to beat about the bush. He always confronted a problem head on. Personally, she would have preferred some small talk to take away the tension building in the room.

"As I explained to Jacey I've been a self-defense instructor here for the last two years. When my grandmother died, I came to Wilderville to take over her bookstore. I came back two days go to finish my contract here. Chase will verify I had business to attend to. I don't believe the location came up, but he knew it was with my previous employer."

"I'll check into that. Do you know Gray?"

"No." He looked towards Jacey before his attention turned back to Kevin. "I know the stories. Wilderville residents are open with gossip, and Mrs. Douglas comes into the bookstore often enough to give me all the town news. With that being said I knew nothing of Jacey coming here. I was as surprised to see her on the beach last night as you are to see me."

Jacey leaned her head back onto the couch. *Mrs. Douglas. She'd die if she couldn't spread gossip about other people. Someday someone needs to teach that old chatterbox a lesson.* She was pulled from her thoughts by a knock at the door. "Kevin, could you get that?" Suddenly exhausted, she closed her eyes.

"You okay?" Blake whispered his hand gently caressing her thigh. "It wasn't my intention to add more tension to your situation."

She nodded. "The tension's been here long before you came into my life."

Richard's familiar voice echoed from the open doorway. Frowning, she opened her eyes and sat forward. "Kevin, is everything okay?"

"I'll be up in a moment." He told Richard before he shut the door. "Blake, I'm going to take your word that you're not here to cause Jacey more problems. I'm doing it because she trusts you. If I find out otherwise I'll kill you myself."

"Kevin, what the hell's going on?" Jacey moved forward on the couch.

"Jay's on the phone. I need to go to the main house. I want you to stay here with Blake. Lock the door behind me." He put his hand on the door handle. "Blake, God help you if you betray us." He growled before opening the door. The warning had to be for show, because no way would Kevin leave her alone with him if he had doubts.

# Chapter Seven

Lightheaded, sickness rolled her stomach. *Jay is on the phone...* She knew in her gut that he wouldn't be calling unless something happened. She tried to focus her breathing, and banish the black spots invading her vision.

"Jacey, you don't know that anything has happened."

Her breath was ragged, and her body shook. Blake put his arm around her and drew her into his embrace.

"Shh." He rubbed his hand up and down her arm.

"Something's wrong...I can feel it."

"You're not going to be able to do anything about it if you get yourself all worked up." He kissed the top of her forehead. "Whatever has happened we'll deal with it. It's going to be okay."

She didn't know how long they waited there. The door opened and Jacey looked up from Blake's embrace to see Kevin's frame in the doorway his face as pale as a sheet, his eyes hollow as if he was lost.

"Kevin..."

"Jay's on his way...he's bringing Jackie." His voice cracked as he collapsed onto the end of the couch. "She's been attacked."

"Oh no." She cried and pulled away from Blake to reach out to Kevin, but he moved away. "Is she…"

"She's in critical condition. We won't know if she'll make it until the healer looks at her."

"Healer?"

Blake spoke up his arms still wrapped around Jacey. "There's a healer here, Crystal. Half Moon Harbor Resort employs her in case there is an emergency. It would take too long to get the ferry or a helicopter in."

Kevin closed his eyes for a moment before he pulled on his mask of authority again. "Crystal is the nearest healer, she's Jackie's only chance. They'll be here in less than an hour. In the meantime, you need to pack. You're moving to cabin three. It's larger and we want you two together. Twins have a special bond. You might be able to help her."

She didn't care about packing instead she wanted answer. "How did this happen? It was Gray wasn't it?"

Kevin nodded. "She was on her way to meet a friend outside of Wilderville, when Gray attacked. Wilderville is on lockdown until Gray is caught. You and Jackie will stay here until it's safe for you to return home." He removed his cowboy hat and ran his hand through his short black hair; a gesture Jacey had never seen him do before. Kevin was always in control, but a fog of confusion, fear and anger clung to him. "Blake you've been appointed to guard Jacey and Jackie as well. One of us will be with the women at all time. You can take over this cabin to be closer."

"Wait a moment. I can stop Gray…"

"Jacey don't. You're not going back to Wilderville, not now at least. I don't have time for it. Now go pack." Kevin's voice raised with each word, his eyes turned a golden orange as his lion neared the surface.

"Come on, I'll help you gather your things." Blake gave her hand a gentle squeeze.

The one thing Jacey hated most about Wilderville was since she was a family member of the ruling alpha she was more protected then other members of the pride. It made her feel as though she was only half living. If she left Wilderville, someone needed to know where she was going, or she had to have a guard with her. The pride women were all protected but Jay's sisters had regular guards for when they left the protection of their community. *Where was Nicholas—Jackie's regular guard? What was she thinking leaving unprotected?*

# Chapter Eight

The tension in the cabin thickened until it could have been sliced with a knife. Jacey paced in front of the window, searching the sky for a sign of the helicopter. Crystal—the healer—sat in one of the bedrooms in meditation, preparing.

Blake stood in her path, blocking her. He put his hand on her chin, urging her to look at him. "You know Kevin's right. You can't go back until he's caught."

"Don't..." The tears welling in her eyes threatened to fall. "Jackie might die and it's my fault."

"It's not your fault." He pulled her into his embrace and kissed the top of her head. "It's going to be all right."

She found comfort in his arms, her head against his rock hard chest. His heartbeat pounded against her cheek. She finally caught the distant sound of the helicopter.

*Jackie.*

She backed away. Blake caught her hand and gave it a squeeze. They made their way outside in time to watch the helicopter landing in the small courtyard outside of the cabins. She rushed towards it and the doors opened, Blake ran beside her. Jay jumped from the helicopter first only to be followed by Meg a moment later. Jay reached back in and took hold of the stretcher.

Kevin jogged up to the side the stretcher just as Nicholas—Jackie's personal guard—stepped out carrying the other half of the stretcher. Blake held her in place or she would have been there. "Inside," he comforted.

Meg moved ahead of everyone to get the door to the cabin. Jacey stood with Blake at her side, tears freely falling down her cheeks, as they carried her sister past. The sight of Jackie's bloody unconscious body cut through Jacey, and she sobbed.

"Let's go inside." Blake wrapped his arm around her waist and guided her to the cabin. Nothing seemed real, not even the ground under her feet. *This is all happening because of me.* She wanted to scream, to fight, anything to get the image of her sister's bloody body from her mind.

Jay exited the bedroom just as they entered. "Jacey, we need to talk. Outside."

She wanted to stay with Blake, maybe explore the desire flaring at his nearness, he was the only thing that kept her grounded. Instead, she stepped away from him, not wanting to bring Jay's anger on him as well, turned on her heel obediently.

Outside she sat on the cold rod iron chair, wringing her hands. "I'm sorry Jay."

He let out a low growl as he shut the door. "That's not what I wanted to talk to you about." He leaned against the railing of the deck directly in front of her. "Damn it Jacey, this isn't your fault. I need to know anywhere you think Gray would have gone. I've had a team check his house, brother's place, and his office. Where would he go?"

"His cousin has an apartment in the city, for when he's in town on business. Gray has a key."

"Address?"

"Johnstown…787 Main Street. Top floor, the penthouse."

* * *

On the deck Jacey stared out onto the water long after Jay had left to make the call to Chase. Her thoughts were troubled, and guilt weighing heavily on her. She should have realized Gray would attack the ones she loved until there was no one left and he could come after her. What she believed was love blinded her. She'd seen nothing, but his lies.

"Jacey, you need to come back inside. It's cold out here." Blake came around the side of the house, to stand near her.

Her gaze never left the water until he put his hand on her shoulder. "How's Jackie?"

"There was a lot of damage. Crystal has done what she could for the life threatening injuries, but her energy is gone. She's resting, and will do more for her soon. Things are still touch and go." He massaged her shoulder and let his words skin in. "She's in and out of consciousness, but you should see her."

She unfolded her long legs from beneath her and stood. "Come with me?"

He nodded and slid his hand around hers. He opened the glass door into the living room. Nicholas lay on the couch icing the back of his head. "Nicholas, you okay?

"Concussion. I'll be fine. He attacked from behind, and knocked me unconscious. I didn't come to until..." Even from across the room she could see there was deep sadness in his eyes. He had been Jackie's personal guard since Jay took over the pride, and they had formed a close bond.

"It's okay. She's going to be okay." She might not be convinced, but she took up the burden of relieving his anxiety.

Meg made tea in the small kitchen and Jacey paused to give her a small smile on the way to the bedroom. Poor Meg had only been part of the Wilderville pride a few short weeks, she should be celebrating her mating instead of being thrown into the middle of their nightmare.

She took a deep breath as she pushed the bedroom door open. The room seemed different, smaller somehow. The bed too large with Jackie's damaged body in the center. The pale blue walls were supposed to bring a relaxing feeling to the room, but it closed in on her. Kevin sat on the edge of the bed, holding Jackie's hand.

He turned when they entered. "She was asking for you. I'll give you some privacy." He kissed her hand and rose.

"Thank you. I'll get you if she wakes. You can be more help to her through this then I can." Kevin didn't say anything as he made his ways past her. *Does he blame me for Jackie's injuries? Will she blame me? I do.*

When the door closed behind Kevin she edged toward her sister. They washed away the blood, and a blanket covered the extent of her injuries. "Oh Jackie." She took Kevin's spot on the edge of the bed and placed her hand over Jackie's. "I'm so sorry. I didn't mean for any of this to happen."

Jackie's eyes fluttered. "It's not your fault. Jay didn't want me to leave Wilderville but I didn't listen. He warned us to be on alert..." Her voice faded off until Jacey thought she had fallen back to sleep. "Kevin told me you were with our hunky neighbor, Blake. You exploring every nook and cranny of that amazing body."

She couldn't believe her sister's words, and sat there stunned. Blake cleared his throat and stepped forward, closer to the bed into the dim light that came from the bedside lamp. Jackie's eyes shot open. Her cheeks became red with the realization he must have heard her. All Jacey could do was laugh.

"I'm sorry." Jackie mumbled with embarrassment.

"Don't worry Jackie. If I had my way, I'd be exploring her. You rest. Jacey will be in the next bedroom if you need her." Her heart skipped a beat and her core dampened at the lust in Blake's voice.

Jacey squeezed Jackie's hand. "I'll be back later to check on you. In the meantime Kevin can get me if you need me."

"Kevin's coming back?"

"He hasn't left your side since you arrived. Whether he knows it or not he loves you."

# Chapter Nine

The long night wore on Jacey. She found Jay in the living room, one arm wrapped around his mate. Someone had started a fire in the fireplace to ward off the chill in the cabin.

"Kevin, she's awake and is asking for you." He rose swiftly and walked back to the bedroom. She wanted to say or do something to eliminate the misery in his pale green eyes, but nothing she said could really comfort him. He faced the knowledge he could have lost his mate before he even claimed her.

"Meg and I are leaving. I have to meet Chase and a team that are on their way to check the apartment. Nicholas is going to stay here as well. We'll be in touch and you can come home once Gray has been eliminated." Jay talked of killing Gray as if he was taking out the trash and that didn't bother her. She didn't care if Gray's days on earth were limited. She only worried he might hurt someone else she cared about before he could be eliminated.

Her brother needed her strength and she did her best to give him what he wanted. She met his gaze. "Jay, I'm going with you. I can bring him out peacefully. There's no need for anyone else to get hurt." She couldn't just stand around and let everyone risk themselves for her mess.

His roar shook the walls. "The hell you will Jacey!"

"Jay, listen—"

He cut her off before she could finish. "I won't hear of it. End of story. I'm your alpha. You will stay here until I give you permission to leave this island. That's an order."

He strode over to her. "I won't find another sister like I found Jackie. Just stay here, your sister needs you, and don't give the guards too much trouble. This will all be over soon."

* * *

Blake watched how Jay handled Jacey with care yet he wouldn't let her get away with something because she was his sister. If anything he realized Jay held her to a higher standard than others. He was hard on her but he respected her.

If Jay hadn't put his foot down when she said she wanted to return to Wilderville to bring Gray down, he would have. There was no way he'd let her risk her life to bring down a man she was terrified of.

Jacey reminded him so much of his sister. Tiffany thought she could change her abusive boyfriend, right up to the very end. It landed her in a coffin. He wouldn't lose her the same way. He had plans for Jacey, and most of them involved her naked.

* * *

Jacey turned the stereo on low to help ease the tension in her body as she unpacked her stuff for the second time in the last few days. Her thoughts kept wandering back to Wilderville, especially Jay, Chase, and the guards who were now hunting Gray. Her former lover was resourceful and proved vastly dangerous. Richard and the resort staff had instructions to get her or Blake if Jay called with an update but this didn't calm her nerves.

She was hanging the last of her clothes in the closet when someone knocked on her bedroom door. "Come in."

Blake entered a mug in his hand. "I thought you could use a glass of tea. My grandmother always said it calmed nerves." He set the mug on the dresser for her. "Kevin's going to stay with Jackie and keep a watchful eye on her until she is stable. Nicholas went to your old cabin for the night and I'll be in the living room if you need anything."

She wrapped her hands around the mug, clinging to it for the warmth it offered. "I don't want to be alone, stay with me. Unless…"

He raised his hand and cupped the side of her face. Their gazes locked and he lowered his head to kiss her.

His lips tasted like warm honey with a spice of cinnamon. She set the mug down before she drew her arms around him and pulled him close to her while his tongue parted her lips. The sweet kiss turned passionate as their tongues met. He raised his hand from her cheek, and ran it through her hair. He pulled back, breaking the kiss leaving her hot and breathless.

He smiled down at her. "I've wanted to do that since I first laid eyes on you, but the timing never seemed right…not that now is the best time either."

"It's as good a time as any. Lately my life seems to be one obstacle after another." She took a step back. She had wanted to feel Blake's lips on hers since seeing him on the beach. Yet kissing him dragged Blake into her problems and he didn't deserve it. It was another person for Gray to hurt to get to her. Her thoughts becoming too much she stepped back out of his embrace.

"What is it?" When she didn't answer, he advanced towards her until he had her cornered against the wall. "I can feel your anguish but I don't understand why. Crystal said Jackie's going to be fine. By tomorrow evening she'll be completely healed."

"It's not Jackie. I know she's going to be fine. I'm sorry Blake, I didn't mean to get you involved with all this."

He ran his finger down her jawline to her chin. "There's nothing to be sorry for. I'm here because I want to be. None of this is your fault."

Her lips curled down in sadness as she wished there was another way. She didn't want to push him away but she didn't know how else to protect him. "To care for you gives Gray another person to hurt to get back at me."

"Nothing's going to happen to me, and I won't let anything happened to you either. Stop worrying Jay and the guards will take care of Gray before he can cause anyone else harm." He ran his hand down her arm, and lowered his head to continue where they stopped. He leaned into her, his mouth temptingly close. "Forget about it for now. Tonight just enjoy what's between us."

His lips crushed against hers. Throwing caution to the wind she wrapped her arms around his neck, and cupped the back of his head to drag him closer. She hitched her legs tight against his hips, her back against the wall. Their bodies rubbed together.

She grabbed his t-shirt and tugged it up. She leaned back, breaking their kiss. "You're wearing too many clothes."

He didn't need any more invitation. He carried her to the bed and sat her gently on the bed. He nudged her legs free and stripped out of his shirt. Tossing it aside, he captured her lips in another kiss. She roamed her hands over his chest—it was so much better than her dreams.

Trailing kisses to her neck, he tugged her tank top over her head, before slowly working his way down to her breasts. He drew his tongue along the curve of her bra and reached around to unhook it— he wanted her bare.

He leaned over her, claiming her lips again, before retracing his path down her body, spending extra time for each breast. As he kissed her abdomen, he unhooked the button of her jean shorts and stripped them down.

He slid on top of her, taking hold of her nipple with his mouth. Teasing it with his tongue. She arched, writhing against him, her fingers knotted in his head, pulling their bodies together.

She drew him to her. "I want you." He surged at her invite, spreading her thighs to gain the access she'd desired for so long He slid his shaft into her wet core in one powerful thrust. The air around them began to warm and sizzle.

Their bodies bound together found rhythm as passion vibrated through them, desperate for release. Waves of ecstasy engulfed them, and he roared. She dug her nails into his back, arching to meet his every thrust as her climax neared. Their mouths fused together and they reached their peaks—together. He threw his head back and roared a second time.

Drifting on the waves of release, she realized he didn't officially mark her. He didn't claim her—he could have, but he didn't. Even during their lovemaking he had kept his beast chained. She wasn't sure if she was relieved or disappointed he hadn't claimed her.

* * *

Jacey woke to the sun streaming in through the window's lacy curtains.

*Grrr, seven twenty-three. Less than four hours of sleep. I forgot to pull the darkening curtains.* She stretched her body out to sit up when she remember Blake. His arm draped causally over her body while he slept beside her.

The typhoon of memories from only hours before flooded back. She had tried to reason with Blake that it was unsafe for him to be with her. Gray would never let him live if he knew Blake cared for her.

At the moment, she couldn't remember how Blake convinced her to toss her fears aside but he had and they ended up in bed together. With each kiss, stroke, and caress he managed to wipe her reservations away. She studied him. A longing to run her hands through his shaggy brown hair until their lips met again filled her. He was her mate. The signs had been there sign he came to Wilderville but she denied them. The way her body called to his was like nothing she had every experienced and it scared her.

She needed to clear her head. A swim would do that. She slipped out of bed, careful not to wake him. Opening the dresser drawer, she pulled out her pink bikini. With one last look at Blake, she padded to the bathroom to change. Hopefully an early morning swim would help clear her mind and give her the strength and courage she needed to do the right thing…leave the man she was destined to mate. To leave the one thing she always wanted, what she sought in Gray yet never found. She longed for the kind of love a shifter only find in a mate for too long, and now she prepared to walk away from it all.

# Chapter Ten

Blake trekked across the beach his rage boiled under the surface. Jacey stepped out of water. The sun sparkled on the water droplets rolling down her body. It reminded him of dew on leaves in the early morning hours. Her wet blonde hair hung in ringlets around her shoulders.

"What the hell are you doing?" His voice low, sending a warning through her veins.

She yelped in surprise to find him just steps away. "I would think it was obvious." She retreated a step back from him.

"That's not what I meant and you know it. You didn't tell anyone you were going. I thought we made it clear last night you are to go nowhere alone." His hands tightened into fists at his sides. The dread that he woke up to subsiding to seething anger—thankful that she was safe, furious that she risked herself.

"I needed time *alone* to think."

He wrapped his hand around her wrist. "Damn it Jacey! It isn't safe. You might not care for your own safety but I do. If you wanted to get away from me, Nicholas could have accompanied you to the beach."

"Nicholas has a concussion and is resting."

"I don't give a fuck. You're not to be outside of the cabin alone. Can't you see I'm only trying to protect you?" He clenched his jaw shut to keep from saying something he'd regret later.

She pulled her wrist out of his grasp and crossed her arms. "Damn it Blake. I've never been one to run and hide. Don't you understand I can't just sit here and do nothing? If I would've known that coming here would've meant others would be out risking their lives because of my actions I'd have stayed in Wilderville."

*Stubborn...I'm to be mated with a stubborn woman. The cold hard truth is the only way to snap her out of this denial she's in.* "He'd have killed you."

A gasp escaped her lips, horror written across her face. She might have thought of it, but her actions screamed she hadn't come to terms with any of it.

"You had to have realized that. I heard the condition he left you in after the last *incident*. Shit Jacey, you nearly died."

"I can take care of myself." Her lips pursed, but she wouldn't meet his gaze. "I've heard the lecture from Jay and Jackie. I don't need it from you to."

He looked off at the water and bottled his anger. Jacey wasn't one who would do what someone wanted because they were anger. No, she needed to be convinced it was the right thing. If he could just get past her guilt, she'd realize everyone was protecting her because they loved her, and not out of a duty. "Love, you wouldn't stand a chance against him. He's at least a half a foot taller and has at least eighty pounds on you. But that's not the point…he had no right to lay a hand on you in the way he did."

He pulled her to him. Nudging her chin up, he met her willful gaze. "You deserve so much better. Let me show you." He didn't give her time to reply, and kissed her.

She tasted of the salt from the ocean, reminding him of pretzels rods he favored as a child. She wrapped her arms around his neck while he devoured her lips. He gave her one last kiss before letting her go.

Richard walked across the beach towards them. He suppressed the growl working its way up his throat. He didn't want Richard the player anywhere near his mate. "Jackie has asked for you Jacey."

"Okay." She stepped out of Blake's grasp and he longed to draw her back against his body.

Nicholas waited at the foot of the path. "Go ahead with Nicholas. I need to speak with Richard and I'll be up."

As soon as she was beyond hearing range, he rounded on Richard. "I see how you look at her. Leave her alone."

Richard's eyes narrowed. "What is it to you?"

"She's my mate." He growled.

"You haven't claimed her. Therefore she is fair game." He turned and moved towards the path.

"You make an advance on her and it will be seen as a challenge." Richard worked his way through vacationers as others ate a meal. His horny wolf demanded to be satisfied until he found his mate. None of that mattered to Blake. Even if Jacey wasn't his mate he'd be damned if he let Richard get his dirty paws on her.

# Chapter Eleven

"Jacey, what happened with Kevin? He sits here by my side hour after hour, yet he won't speak to me. When I ask him a question, I get nothing but a few words. Things were always so easy between us. The friendship we shared is gone, and I don't understand why." Jackie still rested in bed and her color returned. The healer, Crystal, was a true gift.

"I think he's coming to terms with the fact we almost lost you. The news hit him hard. He could have lost you before he had the opportunity to claim you. Give him time." Jacey sat on the edge of the bed, so glad her sister seemed to be her old self. Feisty as ever.

"Give him time? Time to what? Deny what's between us? If anything, what happened served to wake me up. I can't sit around waiting for him forever. We're destined to be together and he needs to accept that."

"What do you want him to do, claim you while you're still recovering?" Jacey tried to laugh it off but she had a nagging feeling that is exactly what she wanted.

"Yes." Jackie scouted up in the bed to a sitting position. "After the attack, I didn't know if I'd make it. I lost so much blood, and I was so cold. All I could think about was Kevin. I wanted him there with me, to feel his touch one last time. To feel his lips on mine. Nicholas was there, I remember him telling me each time I called out for Kevin he'd be there soon. But damn it I've known for over a year he was my mate, and he had to have known longer than that. I shouldn't have had to wait all this time and I sure the heck shouldn't have to wait any longer."

"You need to tell him that. He's suppressed his mating urges because he believes there are too many differences. Show him your differences don't matter, that you can work through anything and he'll step up and claim you as his mate. He loves you but his position in the pride puts you in danger. He's one of Jay's most trusted guards." While she spoke Jacey used the towel, she'd grabbed on the way to see Jackie to dry her hair.

Jackie let out a small laugh, her lips curling into a halfhearted smile. "We're Jay's sisters I don't think it brings more danger than that. If his position is the reason he hasn't claimed me, it's an excuse." She slammed her hand down on the bed. "Enough about my issues. Tell me what's happening with you and Blake." She wiggled her eyebrow suggestively.

"Oh Jackie, I don't know." She dropped the towel into her lap with a frown.

"How do you not know? You haven't been moping around here because of what happened have you?" When she didn't say anything Jackie added. "Oh tell me you haven't. Jacey this isn't your fault."

"I wish everyone would quit saying that. It is my fault. I'm the one who brought Gray into our lives. If it wasn't for me none of this would have happened." When her sister opened her mouth to say something, she held up her hand. "As for Blake, I don't want him to get hurt because of Gray."

"Jay's going to take care of Gray. Stop worrying about it. Has he made his claim known?" When Jacey raised her eyebrow in question, Jackie added. "I know he's your mate. I can smell him on you. But the mating hasn't completed yet. What are you waiting for?"

"For everything to be over. For Gray to be out of our lives." She looked down at the towel, sadness overwhelming her. *How long until this is all over?*

"Don't wait. You don't know how long that will take. Don't let Gray still have control over you. We're safe here, and Jay will make it safe for us to return home soon. In the meantime, enjoy our time here. Go to Blake make your mating official. As you leave, send Kevin in. I need to have a discussion with him."

\* \* \*

Jacey sat on the back deck overlooking the ocean with her favorite paperback in hand. The book lay open in her lap but she hadn't turned a page since retreating out here. Her thoughts were on what Jackie said. *I'm pushing Blake away because of Gray, but I don't know if he'll ever be caught. Could I continue denying him if I knew Gray would be a threat in six months? A year?*

She wanted Blake. To feel his hands on her body, his lips on hers. Her body called to him. Her body flushed with the thought of their matting, her core dampened with desire for him. Her lioness rose to the surface, wanting her mate. But her wants shouldn't outweigh the risk. *Jay, please take him down soon. My will's weak.*

Blake slid open the door, and stepped out onto the deck. "I thought you might be hungry." He handed her a plate with a sandwich and sat a drink down on the edge of the railing. "It's smoked turkey, and swiss."

"Thank you. Would you care to join me?"

"I made one for myself inside. I was trying to give you the space you asked for." He wouldn't look at her, instead his gaze scanned the hillside and down to the water. As if searching for something.

"Blake, I'm sorry." She held the plate in her hand, but the desire for food was gone.

"I don't want to hear it. When you're ready, you know where I am." He turned to go back inside.

She put the sandwich on the rail and raced over to grab him. "You have to know I want you. You have to feel my desire for you. It's taking everything in me to wait. I care too much about you to see something happen to you because of this. Do you understand what it would do to me to see you hurt because of Gray?"

"Damn it Jacey. Nothing's going to happen. Don't put us through this on some off chance something occurs. We both deserve this. We deserve happiness."

# Chapter Twelve

Blake tried everything to get her to accept their destiny—anger, compassion, the truth—yet nothing worked. She was convinced pushing him away was the best thing. He couldn't let her stubbornness allow them to miss their chance at finding happiness.

Her wet lips were right there begging him to claim them. Throwing caution to the wind, he lowered his head, and kissed her. Her sweet taste drew him in, and he wanted more. With one simple touch, his desire for her grew and his shaft instantly became hard. His lion charged forward ready for them to claim her as his.

"You're mine." He growled when their lips parted.

"Blake, you're making this hard." She was breathless with desire.

"No you're making me hard. Stop overthinking this Jacey. Just feel." Pushing her against the cabin, he crushed his lips to hers again. There was nothing sweet about this kiss, his craving ruling his body.

His hands slid down her body exploring her curves, as their kisses became hotter. His hands slid past her hips when she wrapped her arms around his neck, meeting his kisses with desire of her own. He cupped her ass and lifted her into his body.

When her legs wrapped around his waist he took that as an invitation. Using one hand to hold her against him, he opened the sliding glass door. He wanted to get to the bedroom before he couldn't keep himself in check any longer.

He stumbled past the couch cursing because they weren't alone and couldn't make love there. Each of the steps to the bedroom felt like a mile, he wanted her naked body against him. His hands exploring her body without the diversion of clothes.

In the bedroom, he kicked the door shut and lowered her to the bed. They finally broke apart, leaving them both breathless. "Naked. I want you naked. Now." He growled ready to rip her clothes off her.

She untied her pink bikini top. It fell to the bed and his control shattered. He was on her like a lion after prey. He pushed her back onto the bed, and straddled over the top of her body.

He flicked his tongue over her dusty pink nipples, one after the other. They pebbled invitingly. Wrapping his lips around one hard bud, he drew it into his mouth. He circled it with his tongue and slid her bikini bottoms down her legs.

His lips locked onto her nipple claiming it with tantalizing possessiveness, and she ran her fingers over his bare chest. He let her nipple slide from his mouth sitting up just enough to strip the rest of her swimsuit off.

She lay beneath him, her naked body calling to his. He wanted to take his time, and make each moment special. He caressed every curve of her body, kissed his way up. Burning passion crackled through him with every brush of their lips. He explored her mouth with a hunger that wouldn't be denied.

Standing, he slipped out of his jeans and boxers before positioning himself on top of her. He placed his hands gently on her knees, spreading them, giving him the access that he wanted. She moaned with anticipation as his erection neared her tender flesh.

His lion clawed at him, tired of waiting. His natural animal urges demanded to release. With his control long gone, he feared he wouldn't be gentle.

"I want this to be special for you. But my lion is demanding his claim," he growled.

"There will be time for that later. I want you now." She pulled him down to her again, their lips met and desire coursed through their bodies. His shaft hardened with thoughts of having her as often as he wanted.

He didn't wait any longer, he slid his shaft into her. He worked his way in and out of her warm, wet core. Her heartbeat speed up and she dragged her fingers up and down his chest.

He slowed as her climax drew near, kissing her deeply. He wanted the lovemaking to last. He enjoyed the feeling of her impatience growing. Their shared passion pounded the blood through their hearts, chests and minds. He savored every touch. They found the tempo, their bodies and souls binding together, and waves of ecstasy throbbed through them.

His excitement took over and he sank his teeth into her neck. Just enough to allow his saliva to mix with her blood and make their mating official. His mark—a small heart—would remain always on her neck letting everyone know she was his. He sped up, driving harder until he slammed home one last time. His roar mingled with her cries of release.

He collapsed on top of her and rolled to his side, pulling her with him. She cuddled close to him, their legs still intertwined. "I love you, Jacey." He kissed the top of her forehead before throwing a blanket over them. He didn't want to move until he had the energy to make love to her again.

# Chapter Thirteen

They had made love many times during the day until the sun sank in the sky. Jacey dozed in Blake's arms when a loud bang came from the living room. Blake's body tensed and he shot up.

"Stay here. Whatever you hear don't come out there. I'll be back for you." He slipped on his discarded jeans and leaned down to kiss her. "I love you."

He jogged out the bedroom leaving her alone with her worry. She slipped out of bed and grabbed the first thing she found, a pair of yoga pants and her bikini top. It would have to do. As she dressed, she opened her senses. She needed to find out what was happening.

She reached her hands around her back to tie her suit when a familiar smell caught her attention. *Shit!* Gray had found her and he wasn't alone. There was at least one other scent she didn't recognize. She looked around the room for something she could use as a weapon. *Nothing*, at least nothing that would do much harm to a shifter.

She grabbed the lamp—at least it was something—tossed the shade to the side and ripped the cord from the base. She swung it, getting the feel of the weapon to make the most of what she had. She wouldn't let Blake and the others risk their lives for her. She might be a female, but that didn't mean she couldn't fight. She held her own sparring with the guards. Maybe they took it easy on her because Jay would kill them if she was hurt, since the first time Gray hit her she put long hours in at the gym. She'd be damned if she was going down without a fight.

Satisfied she moved towards the door, thankful Blake left it open slightly. Outside she could see Blake struggling with another. *Is that Gray's business partner? I didn't even know he was a shifter. Where's Gray? Where's Kevin? I hope he's protecting Jackie. I'd hate to see what Gray would do to her if he knew she survived his attack.*

She didn't have much time to consider it when someone grabbed her from behind. *How did he get in the bedroom?* She whirled around, holding tight to the lamp. Gray wrapped his hand around her throat and slammed her against the wall. Her head bounced against the hard surface and pain burst in her skull.

"I can't believe you thought you could get away from me. I'd hunt you down to the ends of the earth if I had to." He put his head close to her ear. "You'll never get rid of me. You're mine!"

Black spots filled her vision as his hand pressed tighter against her windpipe. She gasped for breath, and wiggled against him trying to get away to no avail. She tried to hit him, to break his hold until her body became heavy, and black spots filled her vision. *This is it...I'm going to die. I'm sorry Blake. At least Blake and Jay will avenge my death. Gray will suffer for each bruise he caused me and for going after Jackie.*

"Get the hell away from her." Like an avenging angel, Jay burst through a window in her bedroom, a gun in his hand. Chase was just a step behind him.

Gray's claws sprung free and cut into her throat. Warm blood seeped down her neck. A single tear ran down her face as she faced a death she feared. *This is going to break Jackie.* A loud popping noise deafened her, and for a brief moment, she thought he snapped her neck.

Gray flung her away and she flew through the air. His shift from human to lion was nearly instantaneous. Another shot echoed the first and she landed in a heap. Her head glanced off a sharp edge and the world went black. Her last thought was for the safety of her loved ones.

* * *

"Damn it Jacey, wake up." Blake shook her, angry with himself for leaving her alone unprotected. If Jay and Chase hadn't come through the window when they had, his mate would have died. He slipped off his shirt and held it to the wounds on her neck. *I won't let you die on me. You're my mate, we're supposed to have many years together.*

"Crystal will look at you two after she's finished with Nicholas." Jay stood nearby while Chase and Kevin dealt with Gray's dead body.

After attending to Nicholas, Crystal's energy would be limited. Gray attacked him before coming after Jacey, and left Nicholas near death. Blake wouldn't allow Crystal to waste any energy on him, and Jacey needed it. Her head wound was serious. "I'm fine. She can attend to Jacey."

"Blake, you've been stabbed. Just be glad he wasn't a shifter, the knife would have gone through you." Jay shook his head and looked back at Chase as he zippered a body bag. "She's in good hands with you. Holler if you need me, I'm going to check on Jackie."

The stab wound on his side didn't hurt until Jay mentioned it. "She okay?" he held Jacey tighter knowing that depending on Jay's answer it could break his mate.

"She's fine. She was feeling confined. Kevin took her for a midnight walk. They weren't here when Gray attacked."

"Blake, I'm sorry man. I should have let you know we were going out. But since you were with Jacey I thought it would be fine." Kevin wiped the blood off his hands with a towel.

"You couldn't have known." He looked down at Jacey, and used his free hand to smooth hair away from her face. "At least it's over. She doesn't have to look over her shoulder worried he'll find her again. She can have the happiness she deserves."

# Chapter Fourteen

Jacey woke to find herself in a strange bedroom, Blake beside her, his eyes wide as if he was afraid he'd fall asleep and miss something. "What happened? Where are we?"

"Shh love. It's just a different cabin. Everything's fine." He ran his hand lazily down her side.

"Is everyone okay? Gray?" She tried to sit up but the room swam on her. She fell back onto the bed, her eyes closed while her stomach did flip-flops, unable to believe she was alive. She vowed to live her life to the fullest, and enjoy each moment with her mate—*her mate*—the thought shivered through her.

"Everyone's fine. You're safe. It's over. Just lay. You had a nasty head injury. Crystal did what she could for you but you still need to take it easy."

When her stomach calmed, she opened her eyes again the sea green walls reminded her they weren't in her room. Why wasn't she in her own room? She wondered. She couldn't remember what happened. "Why am I here?"

Thankfully, Blake understood what she meant. "You needed to rest and they're cleaning your room. You don't remember the attack?"

*Attack?* She closed her eyes and tried to focus. It all came flooding back, causing her to reach towards her throat. "Gray…"

"He's gone."

She loved the sound of those two simple words. "How?"

He moved a curl from the side of her face and tucked it behind her ear. "Jay shot him after he began to shift. It was too late to stop him from throwing you across the room, but he's dead. You don't have to worry about him any longer."

"The other one? His business partner. He's a shifter?" Relief coursed through her veins. She snuggled into him, breathing in his spicy aftershave.

"He's human. Didn't even know about shifters. Richard has him detained until he can be transported back to the mainland."

With his words, her worries faded away. She no longer had to watch over her shoulder, or fear for the safety of her family. They survived. She wrapped her arm around his chest and pulled him to her. She planned to kiss him, but the look of pain he showed when she touched his side had her stopping in her tracks. "What is it?"

"Nothing," His tight jaw told her it was a lie.

She lifted his shirt to find his side wrapped in bandages, blood staining the white gaze. "What happened?"

"It's just a scratch." He leaned forward to give her the kiss, but she wouldn't let that deter her. She leaned away, wanting answers.

"Bullshit. You're bleeding. If it was a scratch it would have been healed."

"I'm fine. Crystal was worn out, but it's healing on its own. In a few hours I'll be as good as new."

She stared, waiting for the rest of it.

"Gray's friend had a knife I walked into it. What more can I say? You've got a clumsy mate." He shrugged his shoulder, and shot her a smile that had her core dampen with desire.

"You're full of shit but I love you."

"I love you too." He leaned in and gave her the kiss she wanted earlier.

"Does that mean we can go back to Wilderville now?" She pulled back.

"Only if you'll marry me."

"Why would I want to marry someone who walks into knives?" She teased and kissed him again, before putting him out of his misery. "Yes. I will."

# Her Cowboy's Heart

A life threatening attack woke Jackie Wilder up. Tired of waiting, her lioness is determined to convince her mate to claim her.

Haunted by his past, Kevin Roberts doesn't dare allow anyone close, not even the woman he knows is his mate. Years spent as a lab experiment left their scars on his body. But when a lioness hunts, his desire may be their undoing.

Can Jackie help him shed the shackles of his past? Or will his scars rend them apart?

# Chapter One

Jackie Wilder struggled to sit up and her head swam. Every fiber of her body screamed out in pain when she moved, but she was tired of being stuck in bed. Tired of staring at nothing, but the pale blue walls of her room at Half Moon Harbor Resort. Her twin sister, Jacey, pushed open the bedroom door and relief washed through Jackie. It wasn't Kevin Roberts.

Jacey, Jay, and she had always been the closest of the Wilder siblings. While the rest of their sisters were off exploring the world, they had stayed in Wilderville to assert themselves as leaders of their family pride.

"Jacey, what happened with Kevin? He sits here by my side hour after hour, yet he won't speak to me. When I ask him a question, I get nothing but a few words. Things were always so easy between us. The friendship we shared is gone, and I don't understand why." The words poured out the moment Jacey shut the door giving them at least the idea of privacy. In a house full of lion shifters privacy was rare.

"Jackie, you were brutally attacked. He's coming to terms with the fact we almost lost you." Jacey sat on the edge of the bed, ignoring the damp spot created by her wet pink bikini. "You should have seen him when we got the news. It hit him hard, he's realizing he could have lost you before he had the opportunity to claim you as his mate. Give him time."

Jacey still struggled with finding her mate at such an inopportune time. She wasn't prepared to accept Blake until her abusive ex Gray was completely out of her life and the only way that would happen was with his death.

"Give him time? Time to what? Deny what's between us? I can't sit around waiting for him forever. We're supposed to be—destined to be together and he needs to *accept* that." The pain of his denial ran through her like ice water. Quickly she closed the dam, refusing to give him satisfaction of tears, yet her heart broke knowing her mate was in the other room denying her. *What's so wrong with me that he would deny me?*

"What do you want him to do, claim you while you're still recovering?" Jacey tried to laugh it off but when Jackie remained mute, her twin raised an eyebrow in question.

"Yes." Ignoring the nausea swamping her when she moved, Jackie scooted up further in the bed. "After the attack, I didn't know if I'd make it. I was so cold. He was all I could think about. I wanted him there with me, to feel his touch one last time. To feel his lips on mine. Nicholas kept telling me Kevin would be there soon." Tears coated her throat. "But *damn* it, I've known for over a year he was my mate, and he had to have known longer. I shouldn't have had to wait all this time and I sure the hell won't have to wait any longer."

"Then you need to tell him that." Jacey took her hand and squeezed it gently. "He's suppressed his mating urges because he believes there are too many differences."

*How would she know why?* Jackie interrupted her. "How do you know that?"

Jacey winced a frown as if she realized she gave away something she wanted to keep hidden. "There's only so much to talk about with your guard. It comes back to mutual topics…you're our mutual topic. I asked him. I was trying to help." She pulled her hand back from Jackie, picking up the towel again, using it to dry her hair. "It doesn't matter, how. Show him your differences don't matter, that you can work through anything and he'll step up and claim you as his mate. He loves you but his position in the pride puts you in danger. He's one of Jay's most trusted guards."

She let out a small laugh, her lips curling into a halfhearted smile. "That's just an excuse…Damn it, we're Jay's sisters his position in Wilderville wouldn't bring more danger than that. As sisters of the ruling alpha, if someone wanted to hurt the pride we'd be high on their list of targets. It would weaken Jay." She slammed her hand down on the bed. "Enough about my issues. Tell me what's happening with you and Blake." She wiggled her eyebrows suggestively.

"Oh Jackie, I don't know." Jacey dried her hair with a towel, her unease clear in the jerky motions.

"How do you not know? You haven't been moping around here because of what happened have you?" When her sister didn't answer, she added. "Oh tell me you haven't. Jacey this isn't your fault."

"I wish everyone would quit saying that. It is my fault. I'm the one who brought Gray into our lives. If it wasn't for me none of this would have happened." Jackie opened her mouth to deny it but Jacey held up her hand. "As for Blake, I don't want him to get hurt because of Gray."

"Jay's going to take care of Gray. Stop worrying about it. Has Blake made his claim known?" When she raised her eyebrow in question, Jackie added. "I know he's your mate. I can smell him on you. But the mating hasn't been completed yet. What are you waiting for?"

"For everything to be over. For Gray to be out of our lives."

"Don't wait. You don't know how long that will take. Don't let Gray still have control over you. We're safe here, and Jay will make it safe for us to return home soon. In the meantime, enjoy our time here. Go to Blake make your mating official. And while you're at it, send Kevin in. It's time he and I talked."

# Chapter Two

Jackie let her head sink back into the pillows her thoughts serving as her only comfort. *I'm tired of Kevin treating me as if I don't exist. Either he wants this mating or he doesn't. No more mixed signals. I don't want to die without ever knowing the comfort of a mate. Damn him.*

A soft knock alerted her to his arrival and the door creaked open.

Kevin entered and closed the door behind him. Wary caution clouded his eyes beneath his white cowboy hat. She drank in the sight of him. Faded blue jeans hugged his long legs and a tight white shirt clung to his chest. She ached to run her hands over him.

"Jacey said you asked for me." Traces of unease echoed in his voice, almost as if he didn't want to be alone with her.

Seeing no reason to beat around the bush, she dove right in. "What's going on between us? You're moving around me as if you're surrounded by egg shells."

He stood at the edge of the bed, his hands in his pockets, and wouldn't meet her gaze. "I don't know what you mean. I've been here by your side since you arrived."

"That's the point. You've been here, physically—but it's not the same. You know that. There's tension between us now. Why?" She wanted to throw something at him. He knew what she meant. Over the years when she'd ask about his past, he did the same thing, and she let him. No more. "I nearly died and things changed. You can barely look at me. I want to know what happened between us. What changed? If you don't have the decency to be straight with me, then leave."

In two quick strides, he walked to the window. He gazed out there for so long she thought he wasn't going to answer. "We nearly lost you Jackie." Sadness weighed heavy in his voice.

"But you didn't." She hated that she couldn't go to him, put her arms around him but her body wouldn't stand for that much movement. "I'm right here, Kevin. I'm *here*, but you're treating me like some job you're alpha assigned to you. Damn it Kevin, I'm not some charge you have to guard."

"No, it couldn't be that simple. Nothing in my life has ever been *that* simple." He slammed his hand down on the window seal. The thump echoed through the room. "I don't let people in easily. But you…you're one of the closest people to me. The idea of losing you…"

"You *didn't* lose me. I'm right here. The distance and this frosty attitude…it's unbearable." Her voice broke around the unshed tears tightening her throat.

He turned his head to look at her. "The world is unbearable, Jackie. Threats surround us every day. I won't endanger your future any more than it already is."

"We can't live worrying about the future. No one knows when our time is up. We have to live each moment to the fullest by taking the good with the bad. Enjoy each moment with our loved ones and claim our mates before it's too late." She hoped the slight hint was enough, but if not she'd face it like a raging lion in a glass shop. He was hers and she his until death they did part.

His gaze jerked back to her, shock rippling across his face.

*Jackpot! That did it.* "Don't stand there and tell me you don't know."

"How…"

"How did I know? You can't hide it from your mate. I know you didn't grow up among shifters, but you have to know once the male realizes it, it doesn't take long for the female to know it too. *I've* known for over a year, but I didn't force you. I know you never wanted to mate, but sometimes you don't get your way. Damn it, I'm your mate. Do you understand what denying the mating does to me?"

A pained look spread across his face. Was it possible he didn't grasp the consequences of his denial? That he didn't know what it did to her? Sadness spread through her. He didn't know. Growing up alone left him with little knowledge of other shifters, and the mating process.

He crossed the three steps from the window to the bed, his pace tense and controlled. "I never meant for you to suffer. I did this to protect you." He lowered himself gently onto the bed—careful not to jerk the bed and cause her discomfort—he took her hand in his. "Jackie, you deserve someone who'll…"

"Stop." She slipped her hand out of his. She didn't want to hear his excuses, or what she needed or deserved. She needed him. "I deserve you. If we weren't right for each other we wouldn't be mated. It's not our place to decide these things. We're mated, we need to accept that. Please stop denying it. Stop denying me."

Heavy silence blanketed them. She wanted him to say something, anything. But he didn't. The time drew on until her eyes began to grow heavy. She couldn't sit there, looking at him any longer without her anger showing. He would rather live in torment, longing for his mate's touch then claim her. "I'd like to be alone for a while. I'm tired."

Grave sadness shadowed his eyes. "I'll be right outside if you need anything."

# Chapter Three

Kevin paced the living room like a caged lion. He fell in love with Jackie the first time they met. Her sparkling personality set everyone at ease, she could make anyone grin no matter their mood. *Her smile.* It drew him in. Her smile lit up the darkest night.

For years, he longed to claim her, but he held back—he had to—he needed to protect her. He never realized that his actions were affecting her. His father once told him the woman didn't suffer from the mating desire until the male accepted she was his.

*Did I accept she was mine without even realizing?* After many losses throughout his life, he'd sworn to never mate. But did he start the mating process without meaning to? Restlessness thrummed through him. He had to get out of here.

"Nicholas, can you watch over Jackie? I need to get out of here for a bit." He slipped the cabin's key into his jean pocket.

"No problem." Nicholas stretched out on the sofa watching television.

"I'm going for a run. I won't be long." The area Half Moon Harbor Resort had designated for shifters to run wasn't far, but he couldn't—wouldn't—leave Jackie for long. Nicholas had been her personal guard since Jay took over as alpha of the Wilderville pride, but Kevin knew no one could protect her as well as him.

The cool night air calmed the raging lion within. He took off in a leisurely jog, making his way down the path past the mystical lake. The white benches and old lamp posts gave the lake a romantic feel. When he first walked past it with Jacey, he had wished she was Jackie. Once she was on her feet again, he'd bring her there.

He made his way to the woodsy area that the resort kept especially for their shifter guests. It gave them privacy as well as a free area to be themselves. It was a well-planned with a number of dens—especially important considering the owner was a bear, climbing areas, access to a private beach area for the selkies that frequented the island. Perfect. Anything a shifter could want.

It was a quiet night, the wind blowing through the trees the only sound reaching his ears. He slipped out of his cowboy boots and scanned the area before unbuttoning his jeans and slipping them down along with his boxers. He repeated the check one last time and stripped his shirt off. His scars were something he kept hidden—people would ask questions he didn't want to answer, he didn't want to explain how and why. He draped his clothes over the back of the bench, and tossed his cowboy hat on top before shifting.

His body painlessly morphed to free the lion within him and he fell forward to land on his paws. He shook his tawny mane out, and leapt into a run. He was freer in his lion form, more at ease then he ever was as a human. Racing through the woods, he took the terrain with grace.

For years after his capture he refused his lion, terrified someone would find him and lock him in a cage *again*. He suppressed the lion within him. Moving from town to town, when the urge became too much to hold back. Even here on the island sanctuary, he kept his senses alert, listening for anyone who might be a threat.

At the top of the hill, he stretched out on the soft grass and basked in the light of the moon. His thoughts turned inevitably back to Jackie. He hated himself for what he put Jackie though, but she deserved better than him as a mate.

His scars ran deeper than just the visible ones. Mating would put her at risk, not only if his captors found him again, but also from him. Years of torment had left him on edge. If woken suddenly he could react without realizing it. No, he wouldn't put her in that kind of danger.

* * *

Jackie stared at the ceiling long after Kevin left, her head in torment. *Isn't mating supposed to be easy? Why is he resisting what's between us?* Her lioness paced within her, wanting to go after her mate. To demand the answers they sought. She sensed his feelings, they were the same as hers. He wanted her. He *loved* her. *So why does he run? Why does he run from me? From our destiny?*

From the first day he came to Wilderville, they had been inseparable. Their friendship formed in the quick tour she gave him of their small town. She helped him to turn his small house a home.

Memories of the afternoon they spent painting the house flooded back. She was busy painting the walls in his bedroom a fawn brown color and he painted the accent wall a warmer brown. She'd talked him into the colors, into marking the space his own.

She snuggled into the bed, her eyes closed, and let the memory unfold. She'd turned to say something to him, but the words caught in her throat as he climbed down the ladder. His strength, his beauty…everything about him called out to her and her heart fluttered.

Entranced, she stared at him until he slipped on the paint-slickened plastic protecting the flooring and fell ass first into the paint tray. The horrified look he'd worn followed by his glare when he saw her watching his misfortune—they were priceless memories. He amazed her.

And she'd known then…known it into her soul. She loved him.

# Chapter Four

Jackie woke to the sun streaming in through the windows lacy curtains. Kevin dozed in the chair next to her bed. It had become a familiar scene since she regained consciousness on the island. He rarely left and then only when Jacey was with her.

When she first woke from her ordeal, Kevin sat beside her, his hand in hers. Fleeting moments of pain and disorientation gave way to the desperate hope that he was ready to accept their mating. It was too much to believe her near death experience had woken the desire to claim her.

Disappointment and loss strangled her when he didn't act. Not once did he make an advance toward her, if anything he was more closed off than ever. Even their playful friendship and flirtation seemed gone. All that remained between them was a cold shell of what they once had.

She watched him. His chest rose and fell with his breathing. There, but absent. He could have been miles away. She craved him, needed him to lie with her. The desire to feel his body tight against hers, her head pillowed against his strong chest—it burned through her soul, hollowing out where her heart should be. For too long she had longed for his intimate touch—the touch two lovers share.

"How long have you been awake?" He stretched, working out the kinks from sleeping in the chair.

"Not long. What are you doing here?" For too long she settled for his friendship, until he was ready to move and make his claim. But it wasn't enough. Not anymore. She couldn't bear to have him so close and be denied the physical and emotional comfort they could offer each other.

"We need to talk." He leaned forward, his elbows resting on his knees. "You've been cramped up in this room, you want to get out for a bit?"

"Maybe later. I'm getting hungry."

"Let me get you something to eat." He rose, cowboy boots thumping against the hardwood floor.

"Later. You wanted to talk…"

The sadness on his face broke her heart. She wished—not for the first time—she could be satisfied with their friendship. *No, that won't work.*

"I've denied what's between us to save you." He held up his hand asking for silence. His grave expression worried her. "Just listen. You're an amazing woman, and you deserve a mate that's able to give you everything. I've never meant to hurt you, or for you to suffer with the mating desire. I fell for you the first day I arrived in Wilderville. I staggered into your town looking for a place to die. My will to live was gone. When I came to Jay's door, seeking refuge and found you. I wanted you then, and I still want you now."

She smiled remembering that day as though it was yesterday. "Then why haven't you made your claim known? Why wait all this time? You fell into my life almost two years ago."

"I can't be the mate you want, and need." He paced away to the dresser, and grabbed the snow globe that sat there. Shaking it, he watched the snowfall on the winter wonderland. "My past…"

"Your past has nothing to do with it. It our future we're discussing." She slammed her hand down on the bed, tired of excuses. She didn't want to sound like a spoiled brat, but either they mated or things had to change. He couldn't sit by her bed watching over her if he wasn't going to claim what was his.

"Don't be naïve. My past has everything to do with it. There's a lot about me that I've never told you. My past makes it impossible for me to have a mate." He sat the snow globe back on the dresser, watching her.

"You never wanted to talk about your past and I've never pushed. Whatever happened, nothing's going to change it. But we can make the future something special. If you couldn't have a mate then we wouldn't have found each other. Destiny is giving us something we both deserve. Everyone has a past, and some are worse than others but that's no reason to give up on love." She tossed the blanket aside, and moved to the edge of the bed. The pain took her breath away but she didn't let that stop her. "Look at Jacey. She's suffered years of abuse at Gray's hands, but she's willing to give love another shot. Finding your mate is supposed to make you a better person, it completes you."

He stood there, silent and stubborn, refusing to meet her gaze. She rose on shaky legs—her injuries still playing havoc on her body—and walked haltingly towards him, braced for rejection. Pausing a step away from him, she touched his arm. "Whatever happened in your past we'll deal with. Please don't shut me out. Tell me what happened, let me understand."

He didn't pull away from her but she could feel the taut coil of his body, but he remained silent.

"Damn it, Kevin. I'm trying here. Don't throw what's between us to the side." She leaned up on tippy toes and kissed his cheek. "When you're ready to tell me what's holding you back, I'm here."

She turned on her heels on the mission to find food. Already the weariness was creeping back into her body. She barely brushed the cool metal of the doorknob, when he grabbed her shoulder and turned her around.

Before she could fully grasp what was happening Kevin pushed her against the wall, his face crowding close to hers. "You opened the dam, I just hope you don't end up regretting it." His lips crushed to hers. She could taste the strong black coffee he favored.

Her arms moved up his body, her hands running along his chest, until she could slide them around his neck, drawing him into her. He slid his between her lips opening her mouth for him. Passion exploded through her. He ran his hands through her blonde curly hair, as if he couldn't get enough of her either. He pulled back, breaking the kiss leaving her hot and breathless.

He smiled down at her. "I've wanted to do that since I first laid eyes on you."

"Don't stop. I want your hands on my body, your lips on mine. Please…" Adrenaline flooded through her veins, helping her to forget the way her body ached with each move. Without further invitation, he cupped her butt, lifting her off the floor and onto his body. In two quick strides, he lowered her to sit on the bed and whisked her nightshirt over her head.

He tossed it aside, and slid his free hand down her waist, until he knelt before her. He angled his body between her legs. She pulled his cowboy hat off, dragging her hands through his short brown hair. Trailing kisses to her neck, desperation coursed through Kevin. He wanted to take his time, but need surged through him.

He claimed her nipple with his mouth, sucking it, his tongue flicking over her nipples, until her core dampened with desire. She took hold of his shirt, and pulled it up along his back, until he tensed under her touch.

"No," he growled, pulling away from her touch.

"What is it? What changed?" He stepped back until his back was against the wall.

"What the hell was I thinking?" His hands balled into fists at his sides. "I can't do this."

"One minute you're hot and heavy for me, and the next it's as if you turned on the cold water tap. Tell me what the hell changed."

Devastated, she dragged the blanket up and wrapped it around her naked body.

# Chapter Five

Pained, Kevin forced his back to the wall. He should never have touched her. Need raged through him. He never wanted to burden her with it but it was the only way she would understand why they shouldn't—couldn't ever be.

"My parents were world explorers. They hated being tied down to any one place for too long. By the time I was six I started fighting them every time a trip was mentioned, I hated the trips until they finally started leaving me at home. First it was with babysitters, but that didn't last long, and I was alone. I never had their desire to travel and being alone had never bothered me. In honesty, I liked when they would leave. It would allow me to spend more time in my lion form. It was a denied pleasure with them around. They were always too concerned someone would stop by."

It had been years since he thought of his parents. They had never been real parents to him. They only had him to help their image. Their friends were having kids, so they believed they should as well. Once they got tired of him, they returned to their nomadic life. He slid his hands into the pockets of his jeans. Taking a deep breath he continued. Baring his sold, revealing his vulnerabilities, made him feel naked.

"I was out for a run—as a lion—when I was captured. I spent years locked in a cage, as they did experiments on me. When they gathered what they wanted from me, I was sold, funny enough to the circus."

"Experiments?" Her eyes bulged with horror, and a tear slid down her cheek.

"It started out with drug testing. Something to do with an illness that affected large cats. They gave me some virus, but my body would destroy it before it could take hold—a benefit of being a shifter I guess, but it only led to harsher experiments. There were a lot of large cats, but I was the only shifter. They couldn't understand why my body rejected the virus when all the other cats became sick with it."

"As awful as that is—and it's awful—I don't understand why it has stopped you from making your claim." She fisted the blanket in a white-knuckled grip, sadness filling her beautiful eyes.

"The scars run deeper than just the memories." From her blank expression, he could tell she didn't understand. "You tugged my shirt up. The clothes hide my physical scars. The ones I couldn't heal because I couldn't shift. If I shifted I wouldn't have been just an experiment on a lion, I would have been the first captured shifter. The experiments would have never ended then, not until my death. As a lion, I hoped eventually it would end." Over the years he had tried to suppress his memories, to forget what they saw, yet they still they haunted him. Reminding him he would never be completely free, not as long as he had to watch over his shoulder.

Jackie uncoiled from the bed and rose. Determination tightened her jaw and she closed the distance between them, blanket trailing the floor. Her scent filled his nostrils, quieting the storm inside him. She cupped his cheek, her thumb brushing the corner of his mouth. Without thinking, he tilted his head and kissed her wrist.

"Your scars are nothing to be ashamed of. Don't run from me because of a few superficial scars. After all this time you should know, they won't change how I feel about you."

"They are there to serve as a reminder." A desperate desire to give into her, to pull her next to his body, and soak up the warmth of her against the chill of heart rioted in his soul. But it would only make it that much more difficult to distance himself later.

"I wouldn't think you would need reminders of the experiments."

"No." He looked past her into dead space. His gaze not really focusing on anything. "I could never forget those. I need them to remind me who put me there—that my parents sold me out. They traded my whereabouts for their freedom."

\* \* \*

*His parents?* Horror turned Jackie's stomach. What kind of monsters turned their son into a lab experiment? "Your parents." The heartache she felt just saying the words, was clear in her voice.

"Yes. They never were much as parents." His voice was so dead, so empty.

She dropped the blanket and wrapped her arms around his stiff, unyielding form. What paltry comfort she could give him, she wanted him to have. Words would never be enough to erase the betrayal. She hoped her love would be enough to fill the void he had within him.

"I'm sorry." Two meager, insignificant words. She had to show him. "Come, just lay with me. I want to hold you." Unwrapping herself from his body, she took hold of his hand and tugged him towards the bed. He hesitated for a moment, and then as if against his will he followed, his steps sluggish and thoughtful. He scanned the room as if searching for an excuse.

The coolness of the sheets sent goosebumps spreading over her legs and she eased across to the other side, giving him plenty of room to follow. But he paused at the edge of the bed and didn't follow. His anxiety clawed at her skin, made her heart race, and the hairs on the back of her neck stand on edge. "What is it?"

"It's too much to risk. If they find me…"

"How would they find you? You were just a lion to them."

"The circus was better than the lab, but it wasn't the freedom I wanted. I took the time to recover, built up the strength I needed for an escape. For weeks I performed, as they wanted, waiting for the time to come for my escape. We were at a fair in Chicago, when my strength returned and I could run. Late after everything was quite, the handlers were asleep; it was time to put my plan into action. I shifted. It was hard as hell, I hadn't been human in forever. I slipped through the bars of my cage and Al—one of the lion handlers—stepped out of his trailer." He sighed, a heavy weight lifting off him as the story broke free.

"What happened?" She sat on the bed with her legs folded under her waiting for the story to unfold.

"I don't think Al knew what was happening, but I couldn't take the risk he'd come after me. I picked up a board that was discarded on the ground and hit him with it. He had always been one of the nicer handlers. I didn't want him dead, just unconscious, so I'd have time to get away. Looking back on it, I know it was a mistake. He must have told what he saw to someone. They hunted me, it wasn't until I came to Wilderville that I found some peace. They might still be hunting me, but I rarely leave the sanctuary of Wilderville."

"Maybe they gave up. Does Jay know?"

He shook his head. "They have too much money invested and stand to earn more if they have a shifter. Think of the tourist attraction that would be, to have the first shifter in their circus. Jay doesn't know, I never told anyone. Telling anyone could put them in danger." He looked down at her, their gaze meeting. "It's why I've resisted this mating. It will put you in danger. If they capture me…"

She grasped hand again, and pulled. He relented, finally and sat down. "It's been years, if they wanted to find you they would have done it by now. We'll be back home in Wilderville soon, it's protected from humans, we're safe there."

He laid back on the bed, his hand rubbing his temples. "It's my choice to live protected in Wilderville, but I won't make it your prison also."

"Wilderville is my home, it would never be a prison. I have a friend, he's a detective with the Johnstown Police Department, he can look into this. See if they really are the ones hunting you. Don't you understand—we're mates—we'll deal with it, *together*." She lay down next to him, and rested her head on his shoulder.

# Chapter Six

Kevin longed to believe she was right. He wasn't his parents—he couldn't and wouldn't risk losing her. The thought of her getting hurt, or worse ate at him. If nothing else brought home her fragility, Gray's brutal attack told him she wasn't truly safe anywhere. She was one of the things that made him stay in Wilderville. She warmed his life. He would never get enough of her incandescent flame.

She curled against him, her breath even as if she slept. The only indication he had that she wasn't asleep was her fingers lightly rubbed over his arm in small circles. Being denied touch for so long, he cherished the weight of her. Her naked body clung to him, making his almost wish she was touching bare skin, yet his scars made him unwilling to take his shirt off.

Each brush of her fingers made his shaft harder. His body demanded he claim his mate. His lion paced within him, the beast not fettered by his fear. "I fell in love with you the first time you opened the door." He wrapped his arm around her back, pulling her closer.

"I think I've waited my whole life for you." She titled her head to look up at him. "But I'm tired of waiting. I want you, all of you."

She pushed closer, teasing his mouth with a kiss. The taste of the strawberry lip-gloss she favored tested his control

After years in his lion form, his beast lay just beneath the surface, always wanting to be free. If he didn't keep tight control on it the beast would break out of the prison he kept it in. A low roar vibrated in his throat and he took control of the kiss, his tongue meeting hers in a frenzy of passion.

He slid on top of her, his beast asserting itself, unwilling to let them pass on what would make them complete. He devoured her mouth, and skated his palms over her natural hourglass figure. He leaned back, breaking their kiss, staring down at her. "It's always been you, Jackie. Always."

He rose, and stripped off his jeans and boxers, but he left his shirt on. She didn't need to see his scars—he didn't want her to see him as scarred. Tossing them to the floor, he looked down at her naked body. Her nipples pebbled, arresting his attention. Kneeling down, he teased the hardened tip with his tongue. She arched beneath him, a low, rumbling purr vibrating from her throat. Violently aware of her injuries, he explored her body, caressing her skin. Sliding his hand across her belly, he delved between her thighs, teasing her damp core.

"Kevin, I need you." She moaned half a plea and half a demand.

He spread her knees gently, allowing him the access he desired. The urge to take her warred with the longing to extend her pleasure, but his animal wouldn't be denied any longer. He slid his shaft into her wet core in one long, powerful thrust. The air sizzled.

His control shredded. His lion wouldn't be quenched until she wore their mark. He sank his teeth into her neck, just enough to allow his saliva to mix with her blood. Fire raced up his spine, unlocking his heart, binding him to her and freeing his soul in one moment of utter bliss.

He pulled back enough to see the mark. Every mating mark was unique; his mark—a small jigsaw puzzle—would remain always on her neck letting everyone know she was his. *How perfect since she completes my soul.*

Savage happiness ripped through him and they found their rhythm, rocking together in perfect harmony. Waves of ecstasy engulfed them, and he roared. Jackie writhed beneath him, fisting his shirt as she strained toward her climax. Their mouths came together, cries of pleasure mingling as his orgasm triggered hers.

He slid off her to lie beside her. She cuddled close to him, their legs still intertwined. "I love you, Jackie." He kissed the top of her forehead, and drew the blanket over them.

\* \* \*

*Finally!* Jackie snuggled with him her arm rose to allow her fingers to touch the mark. The white t-shirt still firmly in place. *Does he still believe his scars would bother me? That I would forsake him because of them?*

"Take your shirt off." She murmured, encouraging him.

He laid silently, eyes closed. She could have almost believed he was asleep except his body tensed at her words. She had to find a way to help him move past them.

"Kevin, we're mated. The only thing that can divide us now is us." She stroked his chest and traced a path up to his cheek. "I love you—all of you—and nothing's going to change that. Your scars are a part of you."

"I'm not ashamed. They just serve as a reminder that I couldn't protect myself. How am I supposed to protect you—my mate?" His eyes still close, his body ridged.

"What could you have done? You were set up. Kidnapped, locked in a cage, because your parents decided they didn't want to deal with you anymore. None of that is your fault. You did what you had to, to survive." She slipped on top of him, the covers creating a tent over them, her hands on the hem of his shirt.

She slid the shirt up slowly inch-by-inch, waiting for rejection. He laid there under her, only when she was moving it past his belly button did she hear the first sign of complaint—a growl.

"Kevin, look at me." His eyes open, anger glaring in them. If she hadn't been able to feel his pain as if it was her own she would have thought it was her that he was angry with. "Let me prove to you that these mean nothing to me. You deserve a mate, just as any other shifter."

He closed his eyes and nodded at her. She took it before he could change his mind. She pulled up his shirt, as if pulling off a band-aid. Deep gouges, as if they tried to skin him, were carved into his chest and long grooves that looked like knife wounds sliced across his stomach and disappear around his sides. She wanted to ask what each one was from, but she kept her questions to herself. It didn't matter how they happened, and there was no reason to make him relive the memories again. Her hand moved up his chest to the bullet wound that marred his shoulder, from the way it protruded out it appeared to be an exit wound. *How did he survive this?*

"These aren't a sign of weakness...these prove how strong you are. Not many people could have endured what you went through and survive, let alone still have their sanity. Most would have turned rogue if they ever escaped." Her hands traveling over each contour of his chest, taking time to gently run her fingers over each scar.

"The ones on my back are worse."

"I'll get to them." She lowered her head, kissing her way up his chest. Her tongue gliding over the deeper scars, while her fingers trailed up his sides. Coming to the top of his chest, she arched over him watching him carefully. "Make love to me again." His shaft stiffened, and she let out a satisfied purr—they didn't have to be alone anymore.

# Chapter Seven

The cool night air whipped through Jackie's hair, tangling the length of it as they strolled along the beach. But she didn't care. Foamy waves beat at the sand, and misted the air with the tang of salty sea.

"I don't want you over doing it. We should head back." Kevin tightened his arm around her waist, and kept her close to him.

"Not yet. I'm fine. I've been cooped up in that room for too long. I just want to feel the wind against my skin for a bit longer." She tilted her head back, a smile spreading across her face. "It seems like ages since I've been outside. I want to feel the sun on my skin."

"That might be a problem, since it's not due up for a few more hours. Will the moon do for now?" He teased her.

The smile he gave her was unlike anything she had seen from him before. It was like a weight had been lifted off his shoulders and for the first time he was actually living. His scars weren't controlling him anymore. In a few short hours, the change in him was unbelievable.

She looked up at him with a raised eyebrow, but continued walking. The sand crunched under her feet as she made her way further down the beach. The wind stilled and the world calmed, the only noise she could hear was the waves beating the shore. She stopped, glancing around the beach. "Something's wrong." She didn't know how to explain it but somehow she knew something was wrong.

"What is it?" Kevin's hand fell away from her waist, his body tense, his gaze scanning the beach as well.

"It seems wrong." She keeled over, as if in a pain. "Jacey…"

"What?"

"Something's wrong with Jacey. We've got to get back." She rose, and started to jog back to the path.

He grabbed her arm. "We can't just rush back there. We don't know what's going on. Let me take you to the main office. You'll be safe there, while I check on Jacey."

"No. We've got to get to Jacey. Something's wrong." She slipped out of his grip.

"Stay behind me. Gray might have found her."

Their feet slid on the dew covered stones that lined the path, making the climb harder in the hurried pace. The path seemed steeper than it had before, but as she scrambled up it, her sore body protested. Each step her muscles screamed out in agony, her breath coming uneven with the pain.

"Wait." He stopped taking her hand to stop her. "Catch your breath. If it's Gray, we need every advantage. Heavy breathing's going to give us away before we can get close enough."

She nodded, trying to calm her breath. Her body screaming out in disapproval with each move but Jacey's life might depend on them. She wouldn't let her twin down because she was sore.

"You sure you're up for it?"

"I'm fine. Let's go."

To his credit, he didn't argue with her. "Stay behind me, and if anything happens get to the main house and stay with security."

She followed close behind, watching their backs. The path was just downwind of the cabin, giving them a tactical advantage. Kevin crept around the neighboring cabin, trying to get a view of what was happening.

"Can you see anything?" A roar echoed through the air, sending chills down her back.

"Chase's here…" Kevin stepped out of the shadow, drawing Chase's attention.

Chase's long legs covered the distance in seconds, while his ocean blue eyes scanned the area. His gun was drawn. "Get her out of here. Gray's here. He's got a partner with him as well. They're in the cabin."

"Where's the rest of the team?" She asked before Chase had a chance to move away.

"Blake's in there with Jacey. Nicholas is in bad space, out font. Richard, head of security, is with him. Jay went in through the window." Another roar ripped through the air. "Get out of here." He took off towards the open window and disappeared.

"Come on." Kevin took hold of her arm, spinning her around.

"I can't just leave her."

"Damn it Jackie. There's nothing you can do for her. You'd only put yourself in danger. Let Jay and Chase handle it. Once I get you to safety, I'll come back. Now come on." He tugged her arm, dragging her along as he made his way to the main house, using the cabin as shelter.

A gunshot resonated through the air, stopping her in her tracks. *Jacey!* She turned back to the cabin. The only thing that kept her from running towards it was Kevin's tight grip on her arm.

He pushed her against the cabin, his body sheltering hers as more gunfire echoed through the air. "Come on. We need to get inside." He pulled her around the cabin, kicking open the front door. Inside he pushed her down behind the sofa. "Stay down."

*Oh God, please let everyone be okay.*

# Chapter Eight

Kevin should have never agreed to come to Half Moon Harbor Resort without his gun. When it came to protecting someone from an opponent who preferred guns it equaled the playing field to have one. His lion strength and speed gave him an advantage over a human, but not over a lion with a gun—Gray.

He was sent here to protect Jacey. That was supposed to be his first priority. Instead, here he was neglecting his duties so he could claim his mate. It just proved once again he couldn't protect anyone. Maybe it would have been wiser to walk away—but that was before. Jackie was his—he claimed her. He would protect her with his last breath.

"Get off me, Kevin! I can't sit here and do nothing."

"Stay down." He was using his body as a shield to protect her if any stray bullets shot through the walls.

"I need to help her."

"You'll help her by staying safe. Jay and Chase are with her. They won't let anything happen to her. You being there would only divide their attention." He pulled her close, every sense alert for danger. "This is going to be over soon. It's all going to be all right."

Jackie held her head in her hands, her stomach in knots. She hated waiting, doing nothing. She prayed her family—both biologically and Wilderville members—were safe. Her body hurt in places she didn't know existed. She locked her jaw, and the pain increased.

"You're in pain." Worry colored his words.

He needed her and she opened herself to his emotions. His fury hit her like the lion breaking free during the transition. He blamed himself for not being there. He held himself to standards no one could meet.

"None of this is your fault."

"I should have been there. We left Blake alone, with Jacey. You two should have been together, and Blake and I could have handled Gray and his companion."

Heavy footsteps fell outside the door on the porch and he shot to his feet, setting her behind him in one smooth movement, ready to charge whoever came at them. He growled a fierce warning.

"Stand down Kevin. It's me, Jay." Her brother opened the door and the light of the moon cascaded around him.

Kevin caught her arm, helping her rise as she groaned. She squeezed his hand and hurried to her brother, hugging him. "Jacey?"

"Gray threw her across the room before I could get the shot off. She hit her head and is unconscious but she'll be fine. Blake's with her and once Crystal finishes with Nicholas she'll see to her."

Relief threatened to buckle her knees. The scent of blood on him worried her.

"It's not my blood." Jay rubbed a hand down her back, calming her like he would when she was a kid.

"Who's is it?"

"Nicholas. Stop worrying. I need to borrow Kevin for a moment, I want you to stay here with Richard until one of us come get you." As if on cue Richard stepped onto the porch behind Jay.

Jay released her, and Kevin pulled her close. She burrowed into his arms, hugging him fiercely. He didn't pull away, even with Jay watching. Relief twined with joy. Her twin was safe and Kevin was hers.

"I'll be right back." He kissed her before following Jay out the door.

# Chapter Nine

Kevin followed Jay down the short path to cabin three. His nostrils flared, a blood trail led to the door.

"It's Nicholas. I don't know if he's going to make it. Gray nearly gutted him." They stepped over the blood trail and towards the door. "Gray's dead. His body is in the bedroom. I want things cleaned up before Jacey wakes."

They pushed open the door to the bedroom, Gray's lifeless body laid there, blood pouring out of his head and chest.

"Damn it Jacey, wake up." Blake sat in the corner his shirt pressed against her neck, the blood showing through the white shirt.

He couldn't look at Blake without the guilt pressing against his chest. Blake sat there, his mate's unconscious body, bleeding in his hands. He should have been there. They could have protected the women.

"Crystal will look at you two after she's finished with Nicholas." Jay stood nearby while Chase and Kevin dealt with Gray's dead body.

"I'm fine. She can attend to Jacey. I won't have her wasting her energy on me when Jacey needs it. "

"Blake, you've been stabbed. Just be glad he wasn't a shifter, the knife would have gone through you." Jay shook his head and looked back at Chase as he zippered the body bag. "She's in good hands with you. Holler if you need me, I'm going to bring Jackie back over. I want everyone together."

Blake's hand when to the stab wound on his side. "She okay?"

"She's fine. She was feeling confined. Kevin and her went for a midnight walk. They weren't here when Gray attacked."

"Blake, I'm sorry man. I should have let you know we were going out. But since you were with Jacey I thought it would be fine." Kevin wiped the blood off his hands with a towel.

"You couldn't have known." He looked down at Jacey, and used his free hand to smooth hair away from her face. "At least it's over. She doesn't have to look over her shoulder worried he'll find her again. She can have the happiness she deserves."

* * *

Jackie paced by the window watching for a sign of Kevin. She didn't want to be in this cabin any longer, especially not in Richard's company.

"Doll, sit down, let me take your mind off your problems. You're making my wolf eager." He moved closer to her, a spark in his eyes.

"Stay the hell away from me. I'm mated." She paused mid-step, and watched him. *He can't be serious. Even if I wasn't mated, does he really think this is the best time to start thinking with his dick.*

"Mated or not, doll, I can show you a good time."

Her fraying temper threatened to snap and Kevin walked in. "Richard, I told you before stay away from Jacey, that goes for Jackie as well. She's my mate, find your own." Kevin growled, and stalked over to the wolf, menace practically shimmering in the air around him.

She let Kevin assert himself as her mate. She pressed a hand against his back, and slid her pinky in the loop of his jeans. When the tension seemed to calm, she asked. "Can I see Jacey yet?"

"Yeah, let's go."

Outside she wrapped her arm around her mate, coming to a stop. "Kevin, you know none of this was your fault. You were doing your job. Jay ordered you and Blake to watch Jacey and me. Blake had Jacey and you were with me. You couldn't have known Gray would have found us here."

"I know that you're safe, and Jacey's going to be okay, that's what matters." He pulled her closer to his chest, and kissed the top of her forehead. "Tonight made me realize I can't live without you. The scars of my past are nothing compared to the scars in my future if you're not in it. I love you."

"I love you too." She leaned back bringing their lips together. "Now let's go tell my brother we are mated."

"I would rather kiss you again," and he did.

# Marissa Dobson

Born and raised in the Pittsburgh, Pennsylvania area, Marissa Dobson now resides about an hour from Washington, D.C. She's a lady who likes to keep busy, and is always busy doing something. With two different college degrees, she believes you're never done learning.

Being the first daughter to an avid reader, this gave her the advantage of learning to read at a young age. Since learning to read she has always had her nose in a book. It wasn't until she was a teenager that she started writing down the stories she came up with.

Marissa is blessed with a wonderful supportive husband, Thomas. He's her other half and allows her to stay home and pursue her writing. He puts up with all her quirks and listens to her brainstorm in the middle of the night.

Her writing buddies Max (a cocker spaniel) and Dawne (a beagle mix) are always around to listen to her bounce ideas off them. They might not be able to answer, but they are helpful in their own ways.

She love to hear from readers so send her an email at marissa@marissadobson.com or visit her online at http://www.marissadobson.com.

# Other Books by Marissa Dobson

Tiger Time

The Tiger's Heart

Tigress for Two

Night with a Tiger

Storm Queen

Snowy Fate

Sarah's Fate

Mason's Fate

As Fate Would Have It

Learning to Live

Learning What Love Is

Her Cowboy's Heart

Half Moon Harbor Resort: Volume One

Passing On

Reaping Good Time

Restoring Love

Winterbloom

Unexpected Forever

Losing To Win

Christmas Countdown

The Surrogate

Clearwater Romance: Volume One

Secret Valentine

www.ingramcontent.com/pod-product-compliance
Lightning Source LLC
Chambersburg PA
CBHW030256130626
46549CB00002B/551